I0831797

The Extraordinary Adventures of Normal Norman

&

The Myhr of Atlantium

By: Tim Goehle

In loving memory of my Dad…

Ken Goehle

I would like to give thanks to my wife, Sandra, for her support and all the help from family and friends. They helped make a dream become a reality.

Chapter One

The darkness of the ocean swallowed the men as they descended into the depths. The five mercenaries held on to special handholds located on the sides of the submarine. It traveled along the face of the underwater mountain. At this point they were a little over six hundred feet below the surface and still descending. If they weren't wearing their unique wetsuits they would have been dead by now. Pressure in the deep ocean can crush a man like a soda can.

"How much further?" James Wolfethorne asked the captain of the submarine through his helmet's microphone. James had gathered this team of mercenaries and led them into the ocean. His employer had hired them to kidnap somebody.

"As long as the frequency you gave me is correct," the captain told him, "we should be over the transponder in close to six minutes."

"The frequency is correct," James said, "just stay on course and stay alert. The mountain may jut out without warning."

"Are you going to tell us what we are looking for out here?" one of the men outside the sub asked James.

“I believe we went over this on the boat already,” James stated, annoyed. “Our destination is the city of Atlantium. It has been kept a secret by the League of the Golden Arrows for centuries. They would do anything in their power to keep this city a secret.”

“We are coming up on the transponder,” the captain of the sub interjected.

“Turn on the forward flood lights,” James told him. Fifteen large flood lights blinked into existence. They illuminated the face of the mountain for fifty or so feet in every direction. The flood lights shined on an enormous black cylinder-shaped vessel. It seemed to have crashed into the side of the mountain. There was a large gaping tear running down half the length of the vessel.

“Stop,” James yelled into the microphone. The sub came to a quick but smooth stop alongside the leviathan. The sub rotated from left to right shining a light on the length of the vessel. James pulled out his personal light and unlatched his hand from the submarine. His weight belt allowed him to drop down slowly away from the sub and into the sand on the mountain next to the vessel. Standing next to it he realized it was fifty feet taller than he was. Soon after he landed, the remaining men dropped down next to James. The team leader shined his light into the gash.

“It’s empty,” he said.

"It would be," James told him, "it's a supply transport and was loaded with building supplies for the city. The information we gathered told us there were five of them used for the delivery. They were lowered by large cranes on the surface and this one obviously broke loose. After the crash they must have moved the supplies into the city."

"Who would bring this thing down here?" the man asked James. "Who does it belong to?"

"Them," James said, shining his light up the side of the vessel. It illuminated a two-foot-tall and six-foot-long symbol painted on the vessel. The paint was starting to fade but you could still make out what it was. Three golden-colored arrows bound together in the middle of their shafts by five copper bands. The tips and the ends of the arrows were bending out slightly. This gave the illusion that the bands were extremely tight.

"The League of Golden Arrows," James answered.

"I have heard of the Golden Arrows before," the team leader told him, "but until this mission I could have sworn that they were just a conspiracy theory. Who are they?"

"An organization with more money than sense," James told them.

"Over here," one of the other mercenaries called out. "There's a passageway."

They made their way over to the large rock the man was floating under. A little up and under the rock was an enormous opening that led into the mountainside. All the men shined their lights into the cave but they could not see the bottom of the entrance.

"Finally," James said, "you two go and get the transport tank. And bring the sea scooters."

A couple of the mercenaries swam back and unlatched the transport tank from the underbelly of the submarine. The transport tank had been specially designed for this mission. It was an airtight container in the shape of a coffin, though it was a little larger than most. It had no windows due to the depth that they traveled. There were two ballast tanks built into the sides of the container. They could be filled with water or air, which would allow the transport tank to easily rise up or down in the water. The men grabbed their sea scooters, which were personal propelled transports for each man. They resembled small aerodynamic tubes with fans that sucked water in and pushed it out the back end of the device. This allowed the men to travel quickly under the water without exerting too much energy.

The two men swam next to the tank, carrying it between them. When they reached the rest of the team they handed out the remaining scooters and helped secure them to each other's backs. James led the way into the opening. The entire team quickly disappeared into the darkness and out of sight of the submarine.

"We must hurry!" James said.

The team swam in silence to the end of the tunnel. An opening could be seen thirty yards away. They broke through the surface of the water with perfect stealth. James looked around to make sure that no one had seen them. The men left the water and stowed the transport tank behind some rocks that surrounded the entrance to the water. They still had fifty more yards to the mouth of the eastern tunnel leading into Atlantium.

"Let's go," James whispered.

When they walked out of the cave they stared in wonder at the beautiful city of Atlantium sprawled out before them. It was an ancient city rarely visited by human beings. Those who do come are guests of the Myhr, a very old race of underwater creatures that have lived in peace and harmony with the oceans for thousands of years. One of the Myhr, the Matron of the Seas, has a special connection to the waters of the oceans. She can actually control it; she speaks and communicates with the water. Every so often a new Matron is born, signified by the birthmark on her right shoulder blade. She is called the Maiden of the Seas until she is old enough to take her place as the Matron. Then the previous Matron will step down to become a crone in the seeing pool, there she will stay until eventually becoming one with the ocean.

The newest Maiden's name is Meredyth Falworth; she was born just sixteen years ago and soon will be taking her place as the new Matron of the Seas. Tonight she was sleeping in her room guarded by the Matron's royal guard, unaware that James Wolfethorne and his team of mercenaries have entered the city through the eastern gate in search of her.

James led the way through the streets. It became obvious that James had studied maps that showed him the way. He was moving through the streets with ease. They moved through the shadows not making a noise until they came to the corner that led to her house. James poked his head around the corner and could see two guards standing outside the door. They were typical Myhr, tall with pale translucent skin with their eyes more toward the side of their face. Their fingers and toes were webbed for faster movement in the water. The two sentries wore black Kevlar vests, black leather pants and a deep royal blue cloak. The royal blue cloaks could only mean one thing. These were the private guards of the Matron of the Seas; they were protecting the future Matron and her family.

James moved back from the corner and pulled a maroon cloak out of his pocket on his black tactical pants. Maroon was the color that the city guard would wear on their patrols around the city. The mercenaries with James followed suit and put their cloaks on as well. The team's clothes were already starting to feel damp. The air in Atlantium was heavy with moisture.

"Take out your shock rods," James told them and pulled one from his back where it was strapped on. A shock rod is a foot and a half long metal rod with a metal ball at one end and a rubber hand grip with a trigger button at the other. When the button is pressed and someone or thing is touched with the metal ball, 12,000 volts are sent through the victim, knocking them out.

The five men walked around the corner with the eyes held low and the shock rods kept close to them. When they got closer, one of the guards said something to the team. James and the others just kept walking straight toward them. It wasn't until it was too late that the guards realized that the intruders weren't a city patrol.

"Now," James called out and sprang at the two guards. The guards reacted but with little effect, two shock rods made contact with each of their jaws. The guards' bodies immediately went rigid then started to shake violently until they just fell to the ground, unconscious. James stepped over the fallen guards and opened the door leading into the large house.

"Follow me," James called out over his shoulder, "one of you stay and watch for more guards."

The four of them had no more problems making their way to the Maiden's sleeping chamber. They opened the door to see the young Myhr girl with long blue and silver hair sitting on the side of her bed looking at them as they entered. James walked up to her and put out his hand. She looked at him awkwardly at first and then realized that he wanted her to take his hand.

"If you come with me," he told her, "there will be no more harm to anyone else."

She shook her head, knowing that this monster would not keep his word no matter what she did. James sighed and held up his shock rod in front of her. She looked at him with defiant eyes and then made a quick jump off the bed, slipping past James unscathed but not getting so lucky with the other mercenaries. One of them landed a hit on her left shoulder with the rod, sending her sliding across the floor. He walked over and scooped the girl up like she weighed nothing. Throwing her over his shoulder, they made their way out.

When they got to the front door they saw the mercenary they'd left there with a small Myhr boy lying on the ground next to him. James looked at the child on the ground and then back at the mercenary.

"What's this?" James asked.

"He came around the corner and surprised me," the man told him.

"Bring him," James said.

The mercenary that shocked the kid bent over and picked him up. He threw the kid over his shoulder and held his shock rod in his free hand. He nodded to the team leader to signify that he was ready and they could go. They all turned and left the house.

"No!" someone yelled from upstairs as the team slipped out the front door with the maiden. They were maybe twenty yards from the house when the alarm started blaring from the mansion. James and the others started to run back to the tunnel. The shouting could be heard over the sound of their feet running on the stone ground. The city guard was scrambling through the streets in search of the intruders.

It didn't take them long until they came to the eastern tunnel leading out of the city. They made their way to the water and put the maiden in the airtight container. Although she wasn't the Matron of the Seas yet, she could still control some water and send a message to the actual Matron. So they had to make sure she couldn't touch the sea. James went over to one of the mercenaries, named Cyrus, and pulled him aside.

"I need you to go to the entrance and make sure the explosives go off without a hitch," commanded James. Cyrus looked at James; he had a large scar that ran down the side of his face and across the left eye. The low light in the cave played tricks with the tattoos on his arms. The dragons seemed to come to life and moved along his arms. Cyrus was a scary looking man.

"Whatever you say," he told James with a shrug of his shoulders. Cyrus turned and walked off to make sure the explosives were properly placed. James didn't watch to make sure his orders were followed. The remaining men moved quickly and pulled the tank into the water. James knew that the boy would be able to breathe underwater, so he had him chained to the box for ease of transport. The whole team, except Cyrus, entered the water.

Cyrus had just finished wiring the last of the explosives when he saw the guards running towards him. He gathered his gear and started to run in the opposite direction, trying to get out of the blast zone. The Myhr guards were extremely fast and they were closing the gap quickly. Cyrus turned and looked into the eyes of one of the guards, he squeezed the trigger, setting off the explosions. The ground shook and rocked under everyone's feet. Boulders the size of cars fell from the ceiling, closing off the eastern gate and crushing everyone within the vicinity.

Lord Meryck, the leader of the ruling house in Atlantium, approached the pile of rocks that blocked the exit. The Maiden of the Seas had been kidnapped on his watch. Anger flashed across his face as he turned towards the guards behind him.

"Coutler!" he called out.

"Yes, my lord," a Myhr man called out and walked forward.

"The captain of the guards is in that pile of stone. You are now the captain of the city guard."

"Thank you, my lord."

"Use all of your resources," he told Coulter, "leave no stone unturned. No one in this city will sleep until we find her and when we do…" Lord Meryck stopped speaking, his thoughts clouded by anger.

"I understand," Coulter told him.

“Now go!” he commanded.

Chapter Two

Norman Skylair was just like every other normal thirteen-year-old boy in the world. He seemed to pride himself on being normal, so much so that he'd earned the name Normal Norman. He was of average height and weight for his age. He had brown hair and bright blue eyes. Sports, movies and comic books occupied his free time. He did pretty well in school, but he wasn't a genius by any means. He was just normal.

This was going to be Norman's summer. Junior high was finally over, and next fall he would begin high school. He was going to be starting ninth grade and planned on playing baseball, just like his father did in college. He also wanted to join the Junior Filmmakers Club and they had some assignments that had to be done during the summer. This summer would be filled with activities for baseball and the filmmaking. Unfortunately, Norman's parents had some bad news. They needed to go to Europe on some important business and Norman was going to have to live with his Uncle Arthur for the summer.

"I don't see why I can't just stay with Aunt Nora," Norman told his mother. She was sitting across from him at the ancient brown wooden table in their kitchen. His mother, Elizabeth Skylair, was an intelligent woman with strawberry blonde hair and green eyes. She always wore rose-trimmed glasses.

"Norman," she responded, "we've already discussed this. Nora will be very busy this summer. She has taken in two exchange students from Russia. Her house is going to be extremely full and busy. Your aunt will have to take care of five people if you include the exchange students."

"I won't be a problem," he said, "I will stay out of her way. I have all those lessons from the Junior Filmmaker's Club plus baseball practice."

"No, sweetie. I am sorry, but I think that it would be just too much for her."

"C'mon, Mom. I won't be a problem, I promise," Norman tried to explain it to her.

"Norman," his father Jacob said as he entered the kitchen, "your mother and I said no. That's final and that means end of discussion. Besides, I really think that you are going to enjoy the summer with your Uncle Arthur. He lives on a large research boat and you guys are supposed to be go out and do some exploring in the ocean."

Norman's father Jacob was an athletic looking man with dark brown wavy hair. He taught biology and chemistry at the local high school that Norman would be attending next year. His eyes were dark brown and had seen too much of the world for his age. He was looking forward to the next year because he was the assistant coach for the baseball team that Norman was going to be on.

"I can't believe I have to spend the entire summer on a boat in the middle of the ocean with a crazy old man," Norman said.

"What do you mean by that remark, mister?" his mother asked him.

"Sorry, Mom," he said, "but I talked to cousin Lilly on video chat last night. She told me that Uncle Arthur was a crazy old man that spins tales of magic and mystery all the time."

"Well then," Norman's father said, "you know, your cousin Lilly shouldn't be calling anyone crazy."

"Jacob," Elizabeth interrupted him with a stern look. Norman's father just shrugged his shoulders and joined them at the table. He smiled at Norman.

"Norman," his mother said, reaching her hand across the table and setting it on his, "nobody in our family is crazy. This definitely goes for your Uncle Arthur and even your cousin Lilly," she added, glancing at Jacob.

"Hey, your uncle is a very interesting guy," his father added, "he has a bunch of different degrees in science from the University of Hawaii. He has spent most of his life exploring and going on crazy adventures around the globe. I even believe that he was in a few documentaries. He probably could give you a lesson in the film-making process."

"It's just not fair," Norman said, "I worked so hard to get to this point. I was so looking forward to my summer, especially the junior filmmaking assignments."

"I know, sweetie," his mother said, "and we will make it up to you, I promise."

"Whatever," Norman said with a shrug of his shoulders as he got up from the table. He walked away from the table with his shoulders hanging low and his head downcast, "he probably is crazy. What kind of person lives on a boat anyway?"

"Norman that's enough, we have talked about that before," his father warned him, "now go and pack, please. Make sure to bring something warm to wear. It can get chilly at night in the middle of the ocean."

Norman's mother got up from the kitchen table and followed him into the living room. His father remained at the table. She placed her hand on Norman's shoulder and gently turned him toward her. His eyes were glasslike and his face had reddened a little. She felt bad for him. She pulled her son in and embraced him.

"Norman, I am very sorry that you won't get to do the things you want to this summer. We both know that you have worked very hard to get to this point and that makes us proud," she pushed him back gently and raised his head with her finger on his chin. "This trip is very important for your father and I. We will be extremely busy in meetings the whole time we are there. Otherwise, we would take you with us. Unfortunately, you would have to stay in the hotel the whole time and not be able to go anywhere."

"I could find stuff to do in the hotel," he muttered.

"It wouldn't be safe for you honey. Besides, your uncle is looking forward to spending some time with you and he will keep you busy. You are supposed to travel to different cities together and that sounds fun."

"I guess I understand," he said, blinking away the moisture building in his eyes.

"I will tell you what. If you behave on this vacation and listen to your uncle, I will see if I can convince your father to take us on a trip to where most of today's movies are made," she said, "would that be a fair trade?"

"That would be so cool," Norman said with a growing smile on his face.

"Alright then, go and pack your clothes for the trip," his mother said. "And make sure you bring a few books from your summer reading list."

"Okay," he said and turned to head upstairs to his room.

"Norman, I have just one more thing to say. Lots of normal people live on boats their whole lives and it doesn't make them crazy. So can we try to give your uncle a chance?"

"Alright," he said and bounded up the stairs to his bedroom.

***

Elizabeth sat across from Jacob at the old brown wooden table in the kitchen. She was holding a warm cup of hot chocolate, with marshmallows, of course. Jacob was going over that week's paperwork from the Tattered Spine, which was a book store that Norman's mother owned. It was a used bookstore that specialized in old and rare books. It sat at the end of a shopping plaza, where it seemed to mind its own business from the hustle and bustle of the rest of the mall. His mother was just fine with that; she had a loyal base of customers and did a fair amount of business on the internet. The bookstore allowed for his mother to be able to travel and handle legal matters on the side. It had a warm and cozy feel to it, with a bunch of chairs and some tables where you could sit and browse through a good book before you bought it. There was a back room that held some really rare items that his mother had collected on her trips around the world.

"Who'll be running the store while we're gone?" Jacob asked her, "Were you thinking about letting Rebekah run it for you?"

"No," she told him, "it's not that I don't think she can handle it, but I think that she would want to see what is in the back room."

"Oh," Jacob said, "I guess I understand that."

"The store will be closed for a week while my mother makes her way here. I also need that week for Nora to relocate some of the more dangerous items from the back room," Elizabeth said

"Do you think that is truly necessary?" Jacob asked.

"If things are truly as bad as we are led to believe then there is no better person then Nora and her husband James to protect those artifacts. They are both trained protectors of the Golden Arrows."

"I agree," Jacob said, "I still cannot believe that Tessa Tidswell is leaving Edinburg for our bookstore. I am truly impressed."

"I talked to her yesterday to make the final arrangements and she actually sounded very excited about the travel, plus Nora will be stopping down a few times to see her."

"Wow," was all that Jacob could muster up. He bent his head down and got back to looking through the ledger for the store. Elizabeth was playing with her hair while she stared off into nothingness when Jacob looked back up at her.

"What's wrong?" he asked her.

"Nothing," she said

“Okay,” he replied.

“Well it’s just that I feel horrible that Norman is missing out on the summer he was hoping to have.”

“He’ll still have a good summer with Arthur.”

“I know he’ll have a great time,” she told him, “but I was thinking that maybe we can make it up to him when we return.”

“I’m just guessing here but I believe you already have something in mind.”

“As a matter of fact, I do,” she said with a playful devious smile on her face, “I was thinking that we could take him to Hollywood. Maybe even do some back lot tours at the big movie studios?”

“That’s quite a trip,” he said, wide-eyed, “and probably very expensive.”

“I know,” she said, getting up and walking towards Jacob, “but we usually do something as a family for the summer and I think he’s worth it.” She bent down and kissed him. “Think about it,” she said, and then she turned and walked out of the room.

***

Norman threw his old moss green duffle bag onto the bed. It was his grandfather's from his Army days. He drove a tank and from what his dad said, his grandfather was there when the WWII ended. Norman started to fill it with multiple pairs of cargo shorts and pants. Then he gathered up all of his favorite t-shirts; they all had either some kind of comic book hero or video game logo on them. Just in case it got cold, he also threw in his Green Lantern sweatshirt. He also took the large stack of the newest comic books he was saving for the summer and a few good books from the reading list. He really enjoyed a good fantasy book about knights, goblins, elves and tons of magic.

He jumped onto his bed after packing his bag and grabbed his controller. He played his favorite game, 'Red Dragon Alliance'. Norman spent the next couple of hours hacking his way through hordes of goblins and ogres in search of magical treasures and enough gold to fill the keep he had earned two levels ago. After he got his fill of plundering the deep dungeons of Darken Keep, he grabbed his newest comic book and turned on the reading lamp by his bed. Slowly he faded away to sleep while reading his comic, not knowing the adventure that awaited him this summer.

Chapter Three

Norman gazed out the rear window of his dad's dark grey SUV as it drove away from his house. The blue two-story wood frame house never seemed to fit in with other Florida homes, but it was Norman's home. It was a shade of blue that would resemble grey when the sunlight hit it just right. The front door was bright white just like the trim of the house. A porch wrapped around the front of the house and a turret pointed high into the sky on the right front corner. Even though the house sits in the Sunshine State, there are two chimneys that run up each end of the house.

"I feel like I'll never see the house again," Norman grumbled.

"Don't be silly," his mother told him, "you will be back at the end of the summer."

"Just a weird feeling I have," he said to them.

"Well, shake that feeling off, buddy, and don't worry about it," his dad encouraged him.

"How long until we get there?" Norman asked turning back towards the front.

"About forty minutes," his father said, "your uncle's boat is moored at the Symack Marina and Aquarium. I think he has been letting them use his boat. It is a research boat after all."

"Are you sure the aquarium doesn't need the boat still?" Norman asked, "If Aunt Nora is unable to take me I could always stay with Uncle William."

"Now who's crazy?" his dad asked. "My brother William lives outside Buffalo, New York. No, Norman, you will be staying with your Uncle Arthur on the *Sandra Gale*."

"The *Sandra Gale*?" Norman asked.

"It's the name of his boat," his mother said. "Son, most people name their boats."

Norman sat in silence for the rest of the trip to his uncle's boat. The highway was abnormally empty today. It was as if there was something clearing the way for Norman. The sun shined through the window onto his face and he could see his reflection in the window.

After thirty minutes of driving they finally arrived at the aquarium. The tires of the SUV crunched as it drove onto the gravel road leading to the piers. They pulled into an empty slot in the makeshift parking lot. Norman looked around the area but couldn't see the ship yet. The only pier he could see disappeared through the overgrowth, hiding any ship that might be docked there.

Norman slid out of the back seat and landed on the gravel. The heat hit his face like a solid wall, causing him to sigh. The smell of salt water and fish overwhelmed his nose. The combination of the heat and overwhelming smell was not a good first impression! He grabbed his grandfather's old green army bag and closed the door. He was following his parents over to the pier when he heard the chirping of the SUV locking. His fate had been sealed, he thought to himself.

"I can't see the boat," Norman said, "maybe he had to leave."

"It's here," his father said, "trust me."

His parents were the first to push through the bushes. Norman followed behind his parents and looked around his father. Then he saw the huge metal boat sitting at the end of the pier. It was black at the waterline, painted red above that and the super structure that housed the bridge that towered off the main deck was dirty white. She was long, a lot longer than Norman was expecting it to be. "It's probably close to eighty feet long," Norman thought to himself. It had a small crane at the aft end just above what looked like a small submarine. Norman also noticed that it was the only vessel on the pier.

"Is that a submarine on the back end of the boat?" Norman asked, starting to feel some excitement but not wanting to show it.

"Yep," is all his father said with a weird smile on his face.

As they got closer, the size of the ship really started to dawn on Norman. He couldn't even see the harbor on the other side of it. All they could see was a lot of boat and unfortunately a bunch of rust spots too.

"So what do you think, buddy?" his dad asked, "This, is the *Sandra Gale*," he added,spreading his arms wide like a car salesman.

"I'm glad that I got my tetanus shot already," Norman told his father.

His mother was unable to stop herself from laughing a little. His dad just shook his head and looked back at Norman. Then something caught his father's eye. A smile spread across his dad's face and one eyebrow just lifted up.

"Here he comes," his father said. He pointed down to the end of the pier from where they came. Norman and his mother turned around to see Uncle Arthur. A strange old man stumbled down the pier towards them. He was dragging his right foot and leg behind him slightly. He had long straight black hair with a grizzled beard that covered his face. Norman was wondering if he was imagining the patch on his uncle's right eye. As his uncle got closer he realized it was real and Norman just shook his head.

"Is he a pirate?" Norman asked his father.

"Not that I remember," his fathered said. He gave a strange look to Elizabeth, who returned one to him, "but it has been a while since I've last seen him."

"People change, I guess," Norman said with a shrug of his shoulders.

It took a while for his uncle the pirate to hobble his way to them. Arthur looked at the boy with his good eye. Norman just looked down at his feet and didn't want to look back up at his uncle.

"Is this the boy that you warned me about, brother?" Arthur asked Jacob in some strange pirate voice straight from the Caribbean.

"You warned him about me?" Norman inquired with a sideward glance at his father.

"This is your nephew, Norman," Jacob told his brother, with a smile.

"Alrighty, you land lubber," Arthur said and looked back down at Norman again, "why don't you say fairwinds to your folks, lad. Then you can go aboard and grab yourself a bunk. I believe your parents need to be leaving if they are going to catch their plane."

Norman just sighed and gave his mother a hug. She held onto him a little longer than he would usually like but this time he let her. A small tear formed in the corner of her eye and she sniffled a little. She was going to miss him very much and Norman was going to miss her as well. So he just held on a little longer with her.

"Behave, okay, sweetie?" she told him.

"I will," he said. "How long until you come back?"

"It won't be too long, only two or maybe three weeks at the longest."

"Come and give me a hug too, son," his father said, kneeling down to hug him. His father's hug was not as long as his mother's, but it was a lot stronger. It sort of made Norman lose his breath a little. His father pulled Norman back so he could see him face to face.

"Have a good time with your uncle, okay, buddy?" his father told him.

"I'll try Dad."

"I talked with your mother last night. So when we get back, as long as you behave, we will look into making your dream vacation to Hollywood come true," his father said, "Okay?"

"That would be awesome Dad!"

Norman turned around and headed down the pier toward the boat. When he got there he had to walk across a metal plank that connected the pier to the boat. He remembered from stories that he had read that this was called a gangplank. At first he was a little nervous crossing it because of the thin chains that were all that kept him from falling into the harbor. When Norman made it onto the ship he heard his uncle calling to him. He turned around to see what his uncle wanted. He saw him now holding a fake wig with beard and an eye patch by its string.

"Norman," his uncle called to him again, "only go down one deck, that will be the second deck. Do not go to the third deck. It is where the gnomes live and they are a bit moody to strangers. There is no telling what they'll do to you."

Norman just shook his head and walked through the doorway leading into the boat. "*My uncle truly is crazy*," he thought to himself. Meanwhile, on the pier, Arthur gave both Jacob and Elizabeth a long powerful hug. He stood there for a second and got a good long look at his brother and Elizabeth. Jacob resembled his older brother. They both had brown hair with loose curls, except Arthur's was sprinkled with grey hair. Jacob was also little shorter than his brother.

"You shouldn't have said that to him," Jacob said shaking his head, "he already thinks that you're somewhat crazy from what his cousin Lilly said. Then there's the fact that you live on a boat and he believes that normal people do not do that sort of thing."

"He'll be fine," Arthur said with a wave of his hands.

"Thanks again for watching him for us," Elizabeth said, "You're sure that he won't be in the way of your work?"

"Nonsense, we're going to have a great time. Besides the aquarium is busy studying all the data they gathered on our last outing. So they shouldn't need to borrow the *Sandra Gale* for another month or so."

"Good," she said with another sniffle. She wiped away some tears from her eyes with the back of her hand, "we're just glad to know that he'll be safe while we're away."

"He'll be fine," Arthur promised them, "it's you guys that I'm worried about," his face becoming a lot more serious.

"Have you heard anything?" Jacob asked.

"Nothing more than rumors," Arthur said, "rumors about things being set into motion that could change everything, forever."

"What things?" Elizabeth inquired this time.

"We've heard similar squabble from our contacts in the other realms," Jacob responded. "We've no way of knowing what is true and what is not. We won't know anything until we get to the negotiations and hearings in Germany."

"When you work with the Golden Arrows and the Elven Nations it's like you're playing chess," Arthur said grimly, "both sides will move their pieces into place around the world. Then…check mate! So you two be careful over there and God speed."

"We will be," Elizabeth reassured him and then exchanged hugs between each other one last time. Arthur turned and made his way down the pier onto his ship. Jacob pulled gently on Elizabeth's arm, trying to get her moving towards the SUV. She didn't budge. She just sat there looking at the ship, missing Norman already.

"Jacob," Elizabeth said, looking into her husband's eyes, "do you think that Arthur was joking or does he really have gnomes living on his ship?"

"I was a little worried about that myself when he told Norman," Jacob told her.

"I mean," Elizabeth said with a smile creeping onto her face, "it is crazy old Arthur we are talking about."

"I know, anything could be possible with him," Jacob added.

"Poor Norman," they both said shaking their heads and smiling.

"This summer will be far from normal as long as he's with Uncle Arthur," Jacob said as they both left the pier for the car.

Chapter Four

The night was difficult for Norman. He tossed and turned all night long. Strange dreams of swimming deep in the ocean invaded his sleep. He woke with the sun shining through a small circular window called a porthole right onto his face. He was still tired because of his wild dreams. However, the Florida sun did warm his face, helping him wake more easily.

He slid out of bed and landed on the cold floor, making him wish he wore socks to bed like his mother. He quickly put on some cargo shorts and a t-shirt with the Incredible Hulk on the front. He put on some socks and sneakers. Still rubbing the sleep out of his face, the first thing that came to his mind was food.

"*I wonder where the kitchen is on this boat?*" he thought to himself.

It didn't take long for him to find somewhere to eat. It turned out to be only two doors down from the room he was sleeping in. He walked in to find his uncle sitting at one of the few tables in there. Norman looked around at the size of the kitchen. He thought it would have been smaller being on a boat. There were two large fridges, one blue and the other golden. Cabinets lined the far wall and there was even a large oven and cook top. Everything in the room had some kind of latch or lock keeping it closed. "*Probably to keep the gnomes out*," Norman thought to himself and laughed a little.

"Good morning," Arthur said to Norman, "please join me for some breakfast."

"Morning," Norman said.

"There is some cereal in the cupboards over there," he said pointing to a cupboard in the corner, "and the milk is in the gold fridge. The blue one is actually a freezer, not a fridge."

"Why is everything locked up?" Norman asked him.

"Sometimes we hit rough seas while we are in the middle of the ocean. You don't want things to go flying off the shelves while the boat is tossed around on the waves."

"Oh, okay," Norman said, understanding.

He got his breakfast together and sat down with his uncle. They both ate in silence. Norman could hear himself chewing. He was starting to feel a little weird, but then his uncle finished eating and began to talk.

"So how did you sleep last night?" Arthur asked. "Probably not that well," Arthur said, not giving Norman a chance to answer.

"What do you mean?"

"It happens when someone breathes the salty air for the first time."

"What?"

"The salt, Norman, it gets to you. You start to see weird things while you sleep. Don't worry, you'll get used to it."

"Are you joking with me?" Norman asked.

"Wait and see," Arthur said standing up, "it'll be this way for a week or so."

Arthur gathered up all of the dishes and quickly cleaned them. He showed Norman where everything went in the galley and locked it all up. He gave the boy a quick rundown on where things were on the ship also. He explained some of the terminology used on the ship. The kitchen is actually called the galley. The front of the boat is the bow and the back end is the aft of the boat. He told him that if he was facing the bow that the right side of the boat was the starboard and the left was the port side. After about fifteen minutes of a crash course his uncle started to leave the galley.

"We will be leaving for the grocery store in a couple of hours," Arthur told him. "We need to get some supplies before we set sail this afternoon. So why don't you look around the ship and get used to your surroundings."

"Alright," Norman responded.

"This is your home for the next couple of weeks," Arthur said, "so just explore and have some fun."

"Okay," Norman said with a small smile forming.

Arthur turned and left the galley. Norman was thinking of where to go first and, as if his uncle was reading his mind, he popped his head back into the doorway. He just stood there looking at Norman for a second or two.

"I forgot one thing, Norman. If I were you I would avoid the deck below us. There are two tinker gnomes that live on that deck and they can be quite moody."

Arthur didn't wait around for Norman to respond to that statement. He just disappeared down the passageway, leaving Norman alone once again.

He walked to the doorway leading out into the passageway that seemed to run from the bow of the boat to the aft of the boat. All the way at the aft of the boat he could see a ladder that led down into the third deck. He looked back to the forward area of the boat and decided that he needed to see what was down there. He just knew that his uncle had to be kidding because gnomes don't exist in the normal world. So he wondered what his uncle was trying to hide down there. Norman's curiosity was driving him crazy. "*What didn't he want me to see?*" he thought.

"What would he expect me to do?" Norman said quietly.

Norman walked down the passageway leading to the stairs to the third deck. He passed what seemed to be a lounge with couches and televisions. There were two labs in the starboard side of the boat. One was marked "wet lab" while the other was marked "dry lab." All this was interesting, but Norman couldn't get his mind off the idea of seeing what was on the third deck. After what seemed like an eternity, he finally got to the ladder leading down. He stood at the top just staring down and straining to hear anything that might give him a clue to what was there. The bottom steps were shrouded in darkness. A dim light shined from somewhere forward in the passageway on the third deck. Unfortunately, it did not give enough light to illuminate the darkness below.

He took a deep breath and started down. Every noise the steps made caused him to jump. He was just scaring himself even more than he should be. When he got to the bottom he saw a small square yellow light on the wall. There was one every eight feet or so. They were very dim and didn't give off enough light to see anything.

Suddenly Norman saw a quick movement at the other end of the passageway. He almost ran back up the ladder, but he stood his ground instead. Norman could see two eyes looking toward him. The dim lights reflected off the eyes and it reminded him of some scary movies that he had snuck into with some friends from school. He was really starting to get nervous. Whatever was down there at the other end of the boat only stood three feet tall.

“Is anybody there?” Norman called out, not really wanting an answer.

The eyes were moving toward him, slowly at first, but then they started to come a little quicker. Norman let out a little yell and ran up the ladder, barely touching the steps. He tore off down the passageway toward the bow of the boat and up a ladder to the outside decks. He stopped when the sun hit him. Then he turned, looking down the ladder to see if he was being followed. After a minute of heavy breathing and a fast heart rate, he finally calmed down.

Norman stood there trying to make sense of what he had seen on the lower decks of his uncle’s ship. What was his uncle doing with some kind of creature on his ship? After some more thinking he came to the only normal conclusion: It must have been a dog or something like that and his uncle must have been messing with him. Just in case though, he decided to finish his exploring on the outside of the boat. He made his way toward the aft and checked out the submarine.

After a couple of hours he met his uncle on the pier and they went grocery shopping. As he walked down the pier he looked back at the boat and could swear he saw two people looking out of the portholes on the third deck. Norman picked up his pace to the VW van in the parking lot. He really wanted to confront his uncle about the trick he was playing on him, but then his uncle would have found out he had disobeyed. So Norman just climbed into the van and kept his quest to himself. He was sure he would see the dog later while exploring the ship.

Chapter Five

Upon returning to the boat, Norman and Arthur spent time putting all of the supplies and gear away. Arthur had Norman sweep and mop the boat. Arthur called it swabbing the deck. Norman swabbed almost every inch of the upper decks twice. He avoided the lower decks. His arms felt like jelly by the time he was finished polishing all of the brass and stainless steel fixtures. "*If this is how the summer is going to be I might as well stay in my bunk the whole time,*" he thought to himself. Even with feeling so tired and rundown a jolt of excitement rippled through him when they cast the lines off and pulled away from the pier. He made his way to the bridge and climbed into the seat next to his uncle's captain seat. It didn't take long for Norman to drift off to sleep.

Arthur woke Norman about six or seven hours later. It was only nine o'clock but it seemed a lot later. The ocean was black as far as Norman could see, except for a small area off the port side of the boat. He hopped out of the seat and walked over to the window to look out at the lights.

"What is that place?" Norman asked.

"It is Key West," his uncle told him.

"Is it a fun place?" Norman asked.

"Yes it is," Arthur told him, "actually it is one of your parent's favorite places to go."

"I never knew," Norman responded, "they don't talk much about their life before me or where they go when they travel."

"I have a picture somewhere in the charthouse right back there," he said pointing to a door on the back wall of the bridge. Norman looked over at the door and just shrugged his shoulders. Then he just looked back out at the city in the distance. He imagined he could smell the food and hear the music playing.

"Sounds like they had a pretty awesome life full of adventure before they had me," Norman implied.

"Nonsense, Norman," Arthur stopped him, "don't even start thinking like that! I was there when you were born. Your father was beside himself with happiness. They settled down and focused on being the best parents that you could have."

"Sorry, I'm just tired, that's all," Norman said and walked off in the direction of his bunk.

Arthur decided to just let him go and get some sleep. Norman stopped by the galley and grabbed a glass of chocolate milk before climbing into bed. He was lying in bed thinking about his parents and wondering if they were thinking about him as well. Then Norman heard a commotion coming from the third deck. He stared at the ceiling, too nervous to try and sleep right at that moment. He waited silently for fifteen more minutes, but didn't hear anything else.

"This is crazy," he said to the darkness.

He slid out of the bed and hit the floor softly. This time the floor wasn't as cold because he'd taken his mother's advice and worn his socks to bed. He dug through his duffle bag and found the reading light that he had packed. Then he made his way out of the room and down the passageway to the ladder leading down to the third deck. It seemed darker at the bottom this time. Norman knew that it was only his mind playing tricks because it was night time.

Once again he stopped and listened for some noises coming from the third deck but he couldn't hear a thing. He slowly descended into the darkness and turned on his reading light. He shined the light down the passageway but it didn't really help as much as he wanted it to. Everything beyond the light was hidden by darkness. So he turned off the light and decided to go at it with just the small yellow lights guiding his way.

He crept down the passageway trying to be as quite as possible. As he got closer to the first door he heard a rhythmic thumping noise coming from it. There was a large porthole-shaped window in the door. A dim light shined out of the room into the passageway. He really wanted to look in the room but his nerves made him pause. After a moment of wondering what to do he just slid over and looked into the room.

At first he didn't see anything but a huge engine. He was getting ready to move on to another room when a small gruff man walked into sight. Norman ducked away from the window, trying to avoid being seen. After a few seconds, he slowly poked his eye up to the side of the circular window. The man obviously didn't see him. Norman gazed at the little man. He was a short, stubby man about three feet tall. He had a triangular shaped face that got thinner at his chin. Tufts of orange hair seemed to grow from everywhere and course orange hair stuck out the bottom of maroon knitted cap he wore. He also wore a maroon shirt under a pair of denim overalls that were covered in grease. His overalls seemed to have a lot more pockets than Norman recalled overalls having. Tools of all different shapes and sizes protruded from the different pockets.

"Wow," was all that Norman could say at the sight of the little man. Could that be the gnome that his uncle talked about?

"Excuse me!" came a gruff voice from his right and something poked him roughly in the ribs, "staring is extremely rude."

Norman spun quickly and fell back in shock. He tried to grab onto something to avoid falling on the metal floor, but he couldn't move quick enough and he went down hard. It immediately sent a jolt of pain shooting up his body.

“Ouch,” Norman cried.

“Are you okay?”

“What are you?” Normal said loudly in surprise, pointing at the small person.

“What are you?” the gnome imitated Norman’s shocked voice and pointed right back at him with one of his fat little fingers. “Pointing is also extremely rude!”

“Sorry,” was all that Norman could force out. The person that stood in front of him was similar to the little person he saw in the engine room. Except this one was a lot cleaner and he wore a dark green shirt under white denim overalls. He wasn’t wearing a cap and he had golden blonde tufts of hair sticking out everywhere.

“My name is Norman,” he told the small man in front of him.

“And I am Glitch,” the gnome said with a small bow of the head, “and that is my brother Twitch.”

“Are you um…human?” Norman asked.

“Not hardly,” Glitch told him. “We are Tinker Gnomes.”

“What’s a Tinker Gnome?” Norman asked, wide-eyed.

“We are,” Glitch told him.

"I thought my uncle was joking," Norman said. "He warned me about you guys."

"He warned you, huh, and what did you think about some gnomes living on the boat?"

"Really, I thought you would have a pointed hat or something like that," Norman said.

"Hopefully you are joking with me," Glitch said in response. Unfortunately, Norman was not joking but he let out a little laugh to try and make Glitch think he was joking. Norman looked around nervously.

"Where did you come from and what are you doing here?"

"We are from Canada and I am the ship's navigator," he told Norman, "and my brother is the ship's engineer.

"Canada," Norman said. "How's that possible? I thought only humans lived in Canada. How can you be from Canada?"

"We were born there," Glitch told him. "Norman, there is more out there than you could imagine."

"Wait a minute," Norman said, ignoring what Glitch had just said, "I was just on the bridge and I didn't see you there navigating the ship. If you are the navigator how do you navigate the ship not being on the bridge?"

“With cameras.”

“What?”

“Come on, I will show you,” Glitch said and led Norman to the other end of the passageway. They made their way past an old wooden door that really was out of place on this huge steel vessel. Norman stopped and examined it. It had carvings all over it of different people and creatures in multiple different settings. It was so beautiful. The doorknob was in the direct center of the door, with a large keyhole below it. Norman instinctively reached for the doorknob, but Glitch grabbed his wrist, stopping him.

“We do not go in there, boy,” Glitch told him.

“Why?’

“It is Sir Arthur’s private office and library. It’s off limits!”

“What’s in there?” Norman asked him.

“I don’t know. Maybe magical things,” he said with a dismissive wave.

“No way!” Norman said in a trance-like state. Glitch grabbed Norman’s shoulder and gave it a shake.

“Come on, let me show you the navigation room and you would be wise to forget about this room,” Glitch pulled on his shoulder and dragged him away from the door. Norman unwillingly followed him, looking back twice at the door of mystery. Eventually they made it to the navigation room at the front of the boat. The room was literally blanketed with television screens that actually formed to the curves of the wall. On them was projected the outside of the boat. No matter where you looked you could see the ocean around them. If you looked at the back wall it was the view as if you were standing on the aft end of the boat. In the middle of the room stood a duplicate console from the pilot house, with a wheel for steering and multiple levers to control the throttle.

"What is this place?" Norman asked in awe.

"It's my virtual pilot house. I have cameras on every angle of the boat allowing me to have no blind spots when driving the ship. I can see everything around us, even down," Glitch added while pointing at the floor. Norman jumped back a little when he looked down and realized he was standing on a large screen showing a digital reproduction of the ocean floor.

"That is done with sonar technology," the gnome informed him, "kind of like one of your video games."

"This place is so awesome," Norman told him. They spent the next hour playing with the features of the powerful computer. They zoomed in on different images, pulled up charts of waterways throughout the world, and could calculate the exact time it would take to get somewhere around the world, down to the last second.

Chapter Six

Norman told Glitch, "Good-bye and thanks for the tour," then shut the door as he left Glitch's navigation room and headed back up to his bunk. Just as he was passing the large ornate wooden door, he noticed that it wasn't closed all the way. It was actually open just enough for him to slip through. He stood there debating in his head whether or not he should go into his uncle's private room. Suddenly he heard Arthur's voice. He couldn't make out what he was saying or who he was talking with. They were both muffled by the door. Norman wondered who his uncle was in there with. He knew it wasn't Glitch, but could it be Twitch or maybe a new crewmember he hadn't met?

"*Why does my uncle keep all the crew hidden in the lower decks,*" Norman thought to himself and decided he wasn't going to be a crewmember just in case. He slipped into the room. It was dark and very cold. The only light was coming from around the end of a book shelf that stuck out in front of the entrance. It obscured the front section of the room, but he could see the aft section. It was lined with shelves and they were all covered with different things.

When he peered around the shelf he saw his uncle sitting in an oversized red leather chair. It was illuminated by the mirror-like object sitting in front of him. As Norman looked closer he saw that it wasn't a reflective glass at all. The shimmering object was flanked by two large black wooden tubes. These were covered in the same carvings that were on the ancient wooden door he had just passed through. Every few inches there was a brass bracket clasped around the tube. It had two copper hoses connecting the bottom of the two tubes and also coming from the tops of the tubes. The top hoses disappeared into the ceiling somewhere.

Where the reflective glass of mirror would normally be was an illuminated sheet of water. The water ran from the top of the mirror into the bottom continuously. Protruding from the middle was a face. The face was made completely of water and the water flowed over the face as well, giving it an eerie look.

"The situation is extremely grave, Arthur," the face said, causing Norman's eyes to grow as wide as baseballs as he jumped a little, "the Maiden has been kidnapped." Arthur sat back in his seat not saying a word at first. He was just as shocked as Norman but for much different reasons. He just sat there for a minute rubbing his chin in deep thought.

"Lord Meryck, do we know who is behind the kidnapping?" Arthur asked him.

"At this point in time we don't know who's behind it," Lord Meryck told him, "but we have sent our scouts to gather information. We should know within the next few days."

"Do you have any suspects?" Arthur inquired further.

"As you know it is very difficult to get into Atlantium. So at the least it had to have been someone that could pull something like this off. We believe it was either the dark elves or a group of humans," Meryck told him.

"That makes sense," Arthur agreed, "I couldn't see ogres or goblins attempting such a complex kidnapping. Have you contacted the Golden Arrows about it?"

"We have been in communication with them," Meryck said, "and they are going to conduct an investigation of their own to help solve this. It is in everyone's best interest that we get her back as soon as possible."

"I agree," Arthur said, "you mustn't waste a minute retrieving her."

"So if you agree, will you be willing and able to help us?" Suddenly the head snapped towards Norman's location. "There's someone else in the room with us."

Arthur turned around and scanned the room. It didn't seem like he saw anybody in the room. He turned his attention back to the mirror.

"All is well my friend. I must stop in Newport to get something important, and then we'll head to Atlantium immediately."

"Thank you, Arthur."

"You're welcome, Lord Meryck. We'll see you soon."

The face slowly faded away from the water surface of the mirror. Arthur sat very still for a while and looked at his hands. Norman tried hard not to make a sound because the room was extremely quiet.

"You can come out now, Norman," Arthur called back over his shoulder. Norman stepped out with his head down, looking at his feet. Arthur stood up from his chair and walked toward him.

"Are you okay, Norman?"

"I am sorry for coming into your private library."

"That's okay, Norman. I never told you that you couldn't."

"But Glitch," Norman hesitated, "he said never to enter."

"So you met the tinker gnomes," Arthur nodded his head, "yes they are not allowed to enter, because they break most things they touch or "borrow" them for their own collection."

"Yeah, I met them," Norman said with astonishment, "I thought you were crazy when you told me there were gnomes here."

"Norman, I will never lie to you," Arthur told him, "and that is a promise."

“In that case, I could have sworn that you said something about ogres and goblins. Are we going to see any of them? Because that would be really cool! If they really exist, that is…”

“Trust me, Norman, they do exist and you wouldn’t want to meet an ogre.”

“What about the normal world?”

“What do you mean?”

“You know, normal people, like my friends at school. How is it that they don’t know anything about these monsters?”

“Norman, they are all part of what you are calling the normal world. They just choose to remain hidden from humans.”

“Why?”

“Humans don’t have a reputation of treating others with kindness and fairness. So what we call fantastic creatures and mythical beings choose to hide.”

“I would never have thought of it that way,” Norman said.

“Trust me, Norman,” Arthur told him, “it’s better this way. Could you imagine how people would react if they saw a dragon flying down Main Street?”

“That would be insane!” Norman said with excitement, “Dragons really do exist?”

“Of course they do, Norman, but that is a whole different story. C’mon, my boy,” Arthur put his arm around Norman’s shoulder and guided him out of the room. “We have to prepare for our adventure.”

Arthur left the library with Norman in tow. He stayed close behind his uncle. This summer has taken on a whole new perspective for Norman. He thought that meeting a tinker gnome was amazing and he could just imagine what else he was going to see on this trip. This summer seemed like it was going to be anything but normal.

Chapter Seven

The next three days were all the same. It seemed that the *Sandra Gale* was racing against time to get to her destination. Norman spent most of the time on the bridge with his uncle learning everything he could about all the different gauges and navigational tools that were on the bridge. One night his uncle took him out onto a walkway that wrapped around the outside of the bridge. It was called a bridgewing. He showed Norman how to use a sextant and navigate using the stars. His uncle told him that a sextant was a tool that sailors used prior to the invention of electronics and global positioning systems. All this was neat, but Norman soon discovered on the *Sandra Gale* that this was all obsolete because of Glitch's navigation room. So Norman also spent a lot of time there as well. He was still a little uncomfortable with the whole tinker gnome thing, but eventually he came to like them both.

Although the ship was really big and could carry a lot of fuel, they still had to stop twice for fuel. Twitch told Norman that this was only because of the demand they were putting on the engines. The fuel was burning up twice as fast. They stopped in Norfolk, Virginia, and Arthur showed Norman where they built aircraft carriers for the Navy. The second stop was in Newport, Rhode Island. His uncle had a friend at the Naval War College and they allowed them to pull the *Sandra*

Gale into their harbor. As the boat pulled up next to the pier, Norman stood at the bow with a mooring line in hand. As they got closer he tossed it to a young sailor waiting on the pier. After the bow was secured Norman ran to the aft and repeated the procedure.

Arthur secured the engines from the bridge and then met Norman on the port side next to the pier. Arthur clapped both of his hands together and rubbed them as he gazed out at the setting sun. Arthur looked up and down the pier in search of someone but there wasn't anyone else besides the young sailor.

"Oh well," Arthur said, "I guess he isn't coming."

"Who isn't coming?" Norman asked.

"I just thought that my friend, Bernard, from the war college, would have met us on the pier."

"Is this a problem?" Norman asked, a little worried.

"Not at all," his uncle said, "Are you ready to get off the boat for a little while? We have some stuff to attend to in the middle of town."

"Am I ever," Norman said, "I thought you were going to leave me here."

"Nonsense. Let's get going," his uncle said as he made his way down the gangplank. Norman followed close behind his uncle. The young sailor just nodded at the two of them as they stepped down onto the pier. Norman and his uncle walked towards town.

Downtown Newport was the ideal seafront town. The buildings resembled something from a painting of old fishing towns. Most of the houses dated back to the civil and revolutionary wars. His uncle pointed out some large mansions that wrapped around the bluff overlooking the water. He said it was called Cliff Walk and it was covered with mansions that were so big that the entire Skylair family could live in one with room for guests.

It took them a little while to walk to the center of town, but it felt good on the legs. Thames Street was the main street of Newport and it was here that his uncle had to go. They entered into a store that resembled a museum of sorts. It was full of something called scrimshaw, an old art form of carving on whale bones. Norman decided that these couldn't be originals because the use of real whale bones had been outlawed some time ago. Real scrimshaw would probably be in some rich guy's collection.

Norman was standing in front of a display cabinet looking at the scrimshaw. He saw the reflection of an old man standing behind him wearing an old fashioned fisherman's coat. He was dirty, his hair and long beard were scraggly, and his skin looked like wrinkled leather that had been in the sun too long. The man grabbed Norman by the shoulder and spun him around.

"Where are your parents?" the man gasped with a Scottish accent. Norman was terrified by the man but was convinced that the man had mistaken him for someone else.

"Let go of me, I don't even know who you are," Norman said as he tried to squirm out of the old man's grasp. He couldn't break free; the man seemed to have an iron grip. Norman couldn't help but notice that the man had a glass eye. And for some reason the glass eye was green, while the other eye was blue. It was weird and Norman could sense something strange about the eye.

"Your parents, Norman, are in grave danger. The dark elves are not known for an ability to have peaceful negotiations and they are planning something," It was as if the man was warning and pleading with Norman at the same time. It didn't matter either way, Norman was now truly terrified. This man that he had never met before knew his name, and the different colored eyes didn't help. They actually freaked Norman out a little.

"Who are you?" Norman asked.

"Don't worry about that, boy! Just know that I am indebted to your mother, so heed this warning…"

"MORTON!" Arthur bellowed from the back of the store. The man holding Norman spun around and glared at Arthur, throwing Norman to the floor as he spun. Morton quickly broke the stare and bounded out of the store, almost shearing the door off its hinges as he went out into the street. Arthur ran up to Norman and reached out his hand to help him up to his feet.

"Are you okay?" he asked.

"I'm fine," Norman said, "just a little shook up." Norman took Arthur's hand and stood up, brushing his pants off as he looked at the door to the store.

"He knew who I was. And he said that my parents are in grave danger."

"I wouldn't worry about him, Norman. His name is Morton Wolfethorne, his brother James and he were both Golden Arrows. Unfortunately they were steered astray by Mordecai Manchild, a very evil and dangerous man. Soon after that they were pushed out of the league and they followed Mordecai."

"What are the Golden Arrows?"

"They are a secret society, older then I can remember. They have sworn to defend the peace between mankind and the world of magical and mythical beasts."

"Do my parents belong to the Golden Arrows?"

"Yes, Norman, they do."

"Did that man know my parents?"

"Yes, he knew them when they were younger. They were pretty new to the order; you weren't even born at the time. And of course he knows me; he must have seen you with me and put two and two together."

"You got what you came for," the storeowner said, "I think it is time for you to leave."

The storeowner did not seem too pleased by the events that just took place in his store. Norman didn't even notice him walking up to them. His mind was racing about what had just happened and the new information that he had learned about his parents.

"What is a dark elf?" Norman asked his uncle confused.

"I will tell you later," his uncle assured him, "but for now we just need to get back to the boat."

They left quickly and it didn't take long for them to get back to his uncle's boat. He noticed a man standing next to the ship. It must have been his uncle's old friend the professor, because he smiled and gave him a hug.

"It's good to see you, Bernard," his uncle said.

"It is good to see you too, Arthur, but I wish it was on better terms."

"What do you mean?"

"You must have shaken somebody up in town with this visit. Our friends tell me that Fayne has left Providence and is headed this way. So I took the liberty of filling your fuel tanks and had the war college replenish some needed supplies for your galley," Bernard told him.

"I am forever indebted to you."

"Nonsense, I could never repay you for the times that you have bailed me out. Besides, isn't that what friends are for? Fair winds and following seas, my friend." They quickly hugged again. Norman was climbing onto the deck as his uncle came up behind him.

"Just untie us and I will man the bridge. Meet me there when you are done."

"No problem," Norman didn't even question his uncle. He just ran to the bow and then the aft of the boat to pull the lines. Within seconds the vessel moved forward into the night. Norman stood on the deck watching the town of Newport moving away. As they passed the lighthouse on the island, Norman jumped back in shock. Morton was standing on the island looking at them through an eyeglass. Norman stood very still for a while, and then he raced back into the ship and up to the bridge. He didn't understand why, but Norman didn't speak a word of what he just saw to his uncle.

The night had finally come and the sea was very quiet. Norman stood on the bridge with his uncle and looked out across the dark water. The moon was very bright tonight and Norman could see very well from where he was.

"Is something wrong?" Norman asked his uncle.

"Yes, but I don't know what it is Norman."

"What do you mean?"

"There is something happening, something very bad, and from what I can guess, it involves the Myhr and some very dangerous people I know."

"Is it the Fayne guy, who is he?"

"Yes, I am worried about Fayne, but I do not think he would act alone. You see, Norman, Fayne is a dark elf and they usually work behind the scenes trying to manipulate events. They use other people to further their plans and they are usually evil plans," Arthur told him.

"So we are worried about who he is manipulating?" Norman asked.

"Yes, I don't think it is a coincidence that he showed up in Providence. It's too close to the entrance of Atlantium for just mere coincidence and then the Maiden gets kidnapped. It all makes the hair on my arms tingle and that means bad things are coming."

"What are dark elves?" Norman asked again.

“It would take all summer to educate you on the elven nations. So let me just tell you that there are three basic types of elves in the world. There are good elves, evil elves, which are usually just called the dark elves, and there are neutral elves. The good elves live in peace with mankind. They are made up of the golden elves and the earth elves. The dark elves were at one time just the fire elves. Unfortunately over the past few centuries a new breed of dark elf called the blood elves has surfaced. The blood elves are extremely violent and deadly. Few humans live to talk about their encounters with a blood elf. The last group is what we have come to know as the neutral elves. They are made up of water elves and wind elves. They are called neutral because they have been known to take whatever side they seem to think is right at that moment.”

“That’s crazy,” Norman said.

“It is crazy, Norman. What is worse is that we do not really know the whole of it yet. What we know are just pieces of a bigger puzzle and that’s what worries me.”

“So we don’t know what is happening but here we are racing into the darkness searching for answers.”

“That about sums it up, Norman. We must discover the truth and do what we can to help fix the situation.”

"I don't understand why we have to do this, Uncle Arthur? I mean, we are just normal people; well, at least I am a normal kind of kid. I am not a Golden Arrow or anything like that."

"Well, you see, Normal Norman, the world always has good and evil forces pushing and influencing the outcomes. Sometimes the balance is skewed and one grows stronger over the other. That is when someone else, such as ourselves, need to step up and do what is right," Norman understood what his uncle was saying, but he didn't want to agree with it. Norman was just scared about what was ahead of them.

Chapter Eight

The *Sandra Gale* shuddered and came to a halt in the middle of the ocean. Norman was sitting with his uncle on the bridge. It was the second night since they had left Newport. Norman slid out of his seat and looked outside of the bridge windows. He didn't see any land or boats in sight.

"Why are we stopping?" Norman asked his uncle.

"We must have arrived at our destination," he told him. Arthur got out of his seat and stepped next to Norman.

"I thought that we were going to Atlantium?"

"We are," Arthur informed him.

"I don't see it," Norman said looking around.

"Oh you wouldn't see it from here," he said, "Atlantium is under the sea."

"Underwater?"

"I am sure you have heard of the story of Atlantis right?"

"Of course," Norman said, "I think everyone has heard the story."

"Well, the one fallacy is that the city never existed outside of the water. It has always been on the ocean floor, or should I say in, because it resides inside a large underwater mountain," his uncle could see the confusion on his nephew's face. So he continued with the story.

"You see, during the time of its original discovery, no one would believe that such a city existed. It couldn't be understood by mankind how such a place could survive. Luckily for the Myrh, the discovery was made by scholars who were not interested in riches, and they decided that the fate of the city would be better served if it were kept a secret."

"Well how did the legend get out then, if they were keeping it a secret?"

"Just like all things in life Norman, greed reared its ugly head. Two in the group started to think of the financial gain that could be had for such a find. That is when the other three decided to bring forth the story as legend and beat their associates at their own game. All the charts and maps were taken across the ocean and hidden. Eventually their location was forgotten about. Even the people who knew of the city didn't know about the chart's location. So the city was safe, at least for a time."

"That is amazing," Norman gasped, "how can anybody live under the water? Do they have gills and tails like the stories of mermaids?"

“All in due time, Norman. First let’s go downstairs and get some food.”

Arthur walked out of the bridge with Norman close behind. They made their way to the galley to get some dinner. In the galley, Glitch and Twitch had already arrived and they were eating what looked like a ton food. They had plates piled high with cooked meats and potatoes. There was enough food to feed ten people.

“Do you see why I have to buy so much food before we leave port?” Arthur asked Norman.

“I do now,” Norman said with a small laugh.

“What’s so funny?” Twitch asked, “It’s hard work running this ship.”

“Yeah,” Glitch agreed, “It’s not like we get to sit on the bridge drinking ice tea all day and watching the dolphins.”

Glitch nudged his brother with a short and thick elbow. They both laughed as they took their seats in front of the mountains of food. Arthur just shrugged and went to the fridge to see if any food was left for them. He made two plates, one for himself and one for Norman. They took their seats across from the two gnomes.

“We made really good time getting here,” Arthur said to Glitch.

“Well, of course,” Glitch responded, “I mapped out a perfect route. I took advantage of our state of the art navigation equipment and got us here as quickly as possible.”

“Well, it seems your efforts got us here in record time,” Arthur responded.

“That is such garbage,” Twitch interrupted.

“Excuse me?” Glitch said putting his hand to his chest offended.

“You heard me,” Twitch told him.

“That is enough,” Arthur said, “could we just eat in peace tonight?”

“Of course we can,” Glitch told him, “just as soon as my scoundrel of a brother tells me what he means by his extremely rude remarks.”

“All I am saying is that you could map out a flawless route but without the engines running at full throttle, you wouldn’t be able to go anywhere,” Twitch told him gloatingly.

“Well, that makes sense,” Norman said, shoveling some food in his mouth. Glitch glowered at Norman. At first he didn’t say a word he just looked, glaring at Norman. He started to get a little nervous thinking that he may have said something wrong.

“Well, maybe I should let you navigate the ship instead?” Glitch said to Norman, “How would you like that?”

“Can we please talk about this another time?” Arthur asked looking at both Glitch and Twitch.

“Fine,” they both said in unison.

“Thank you,” Arthur said, “we have a lot to get done prior to our guest arriving tomorrow.”

“Who is coming tomorrow?” Norman asked.

“You know, maybe we will let it be a surprise. You better get a full night’s sleep because we have a busy day ahead of us,” Arthur said, then stood up, “and you two quit your arguing. Then go down stairs and get the DART ready for launch tomorrow.”

All three of them watched as Arthur walked out of the galley. At first no one said anything. They just continued to eat in silence. When the two gnomes were finished eating they cleaned up and looked at Norman.

“Well, are you going to come with us or not?” Glitch asked Norman.

“Where?” Norman asked.

“We’re getting the DART ready for tomorrow,” Twitch told him.

"What is the DART?" Norman asked them.

"It's called the Deep Aquatic Reconnaissance Transport, but we call it the DART for short," Glitch said.

"Not to mention that it is shaped like the tip of a dart," Twitch added.

"I am coming," Norman said and quickly cleaned up his dishes. He followed the two gnomes out of the galley and to the aft end of the passageway. This time they didn't go down the stairs leading to the engine room and navigation room. Twitch opened a small hatch to the side of the stairs and climbed in. Norman and Glitch followed him through the hatch. It was just a tube-shaped ladderwell that ran from the top decks to the bottom of the boat. They all climbed down the ladder to the bottom and entered the only door there.

Norman entered into a large room with a pool of water in the middle of it. Suspended above the pool was a large copper and bronze looking thing. It was in the shape of the tip of an arrow without the long shaft coming out of the end.

"Is that the DART?" Norman asked.

"Of course," Glitch told him.

"It's the only thing in the room that is in the shape of a dart," Twitch said.

Norman was used to the way that Glitch and Twitch talked to everyone. So he just ignored them and walked around the DART examining every square inch of it. There was only one hatch on the side and three fins coming of the side, making it look like a real dart. Norman couldn't see any windows on it.

"Where are the windows?" Norman asked.

"There aren't any," Glitch told him.

"How would they know where they are going?"

"There are no windows because they would shatter due to the immense pressures on the bottom of the ocean. Besides, the DART is a self-guiding transport system. You just enter the destination and it takes you where you need to go," Glitch told him.

"How can it go to the bottom of the ocean?"

"It isn't how it was built, but who built it," Glitch told him. Norman peered around the DART at the two gnomes.

"What does that mean?"

"The DART was built by the Clockwork Dwarves under the mountain of Banff," Glitch told him.

"Dwarves!" Norman said as his jaw hit the ground, "this summer keeps getting better."

"Wait until you see what powers it," Twitch told him.

"Well, what powers it?" Norman asked him.

"You will see in the morning," Twitch said as he set out to get the DART ready.

"Awww man!" Norman said, swinging his arms.

"We have a lot of work to do," Twitch said to Glitch, "let's go."

"So what do you guys know about Atlantium?" Norman asked.

"It is underwater," Twitch said to him.

"I know that already," Norman said to them.

"Well maybe if you asked a specific question," Glitch told him. "Then I might give you a better answer."

"Who lives down there and what is it like?" Norman asked.

"The Myhr live down there," Twitch said.

"We don't know what it is like down there," Glitch added, "we have never been there."

"What are the Myhr like?" Norman asked, "Do they look like fish?"

"Yeah and they wear pointed hats just like us gnomes," Glitch said with a laugh.

“Ha-ha funny,” Norman said with a fake laugh.

“We’re just joking with you Norman,” Twitch said, “I do not know exactly what the Myhr are like, but they are definitely not fish.”

“Although they do have gills,” Glitch said.

“And webbed feet,” Twitch added.

“That’s so cool,” Norman said.

Chapter Nine

Norman woke to the sound of something banging against the wall in his room. He could hear people talking in the passageway but could only make out one of them. He wondered if it was his uncle and who was he talking to, maybe Glitch or Twitch.

"Be careful!" he heard a muffled voice say. "If we drop those crystals, this whole ship is going to go up in a ball of fire." This got Norman's attention, so he sprang out of bed, throwing on some shorts and a t-shirt. Then he made his way to the hatch. Opening it and stepping through, he looked just in time to see the top of someone's head disappearing down the ladderwell leading to the engine room. Norman was about to follow when he heard the opening and closing of the hatch leading to the outer decks. Just as it closed he heard his uncle yell out to someone named Noah.

Norman turned and made his way towards that hatch. He walked outside, once again just in time to see someone turn around a corner to the stairs leading up to the bridge and chart house. Norman raced after this Noah person, starting to get frustrated. As soon as he got to the bottom of the stairs, he saw the door shutting and someone's boot as they walked into the bridge.

"Ah, come on!" Norman yelled to himself and the ocean. Norman bound up the stairs, skipping steps, and swung the door open. Inside the bridge his uncle, some big guy and a beautiful woman with silver hair turned to look at him.

"Good morning young Norman," the large man said to him.

"Uh, good morning," Norman stuttered in reply. It took Norman a few seconds to get his bearing but then he started to get curious. "Who are you?" he asked the large man in front of him.

"I apologize, Norman, where are my manners? My name is Noah and I am glad to finally meet you," said Noah, "and this is Lady Meara," he added, pointing to the lady between him and Uncle Arthur.

"They're ambassadors from the court of Water Elves," his uncle told him. "Lady Meara is actually Princess Meara, Norman." This caused Norman to once again to lose his bearings. The water elves were more beautiful than any person Norman had ever seen. Their skin was like porcelain, pure white and it looked as smooth as glass. They had hair of silver with different shades of blue running through it.

"How did you get here?"

"We came on the *Mist Traveler*," Meara told him, while pointing to the large wooden warship on the starboard side of the *Sandra Gale*. Norman's eyes almost jumped out of his head. It looked like a boat right out of a pirate movie. He forgot about the rest of the people in the room and walked over to the window and stared out at the ship.

"That is so cool." Norman said, "This is an awesome summer."

"I am glad to see that you are excited, Norman," Meara said, "but we have much to do to prepare the DART for departure."

"You are right." Arthur told her, "How much longer until the blue crystals are ready for the launch?"

"Blue crystals?" Norman asked.

"It is the propulsion for the DART," Noah told him.

"Let's all head down to the dive pool and help with the final preparations," Arthur said and started to head out of the bridge, when Meara grabbed his arm.

"There is something I was going to tell you earlier," she said in hush tones, "Lady Lilliana is on her way to the hearings in Germany."

"Princess Lilliana!" Arthur said in shock as he stopped in his tracks. "She has been in hiding for thirteen years, what would bring her out?"

"The elves stand on the brink of war," she told him.

"She should not have left," he responded. "There are others that can talk in her place."

"Would you have the Elven nations go to war?"

"It is too dangerous! When the dark elves see her at the hearing, who knows what they'll do."

"It is no more dangerous than travelling with the arrow of light," she informed Arthur while nodding towards Norman. He looked at the boy then back at Lady Meara.

"That is nonsense," he told her.

"What is the arrow of light?" Norman asked his uncle.

"It is just a legend, Norman, a tale told by old men," he responded.

"Legends are born from truths," Meara said as she walked out of the bridge, "you told me that yourself," she called back to Arthur. Norman watched as the elves walked ahead of them. They moved like their feet never touched the ground. They moved so smooth and elegant, yet their bodies were toned and muscular, showing their strength.

Arthur followed them out of the bridge and led Norman down to his private office and library. He sat down in front of the waterlink, which his uncle had used to talk with Lord Meryck a few days ago. His uncle was looking for something on the shelves. He was digging through the different trinkets and artifacts.

"Here it is," Arthur said as he pulled out a small item from a small chest. It was wrapped in an old looking cloth. He turned, smiling at Norman, holding up the wrapped item. He walked over and handed it to Norman.

"I think you should have this," Arthur told him. "Actually I think that your grandfather would have wanted you to have it."

"Grandpa Alistair?" Norman asked as he took the package.

"The one and only," Arthur said.

"What is it?" he asked as he undid the cloth from around the item. A small metal tin fell out into the palm of his hand. It was about four inches in diameter. It was divided into two halves that twisted side to side. On the top half, lined up across the middle, were twenty six different symbols, on top of it were the roman numerals I through IV. On the bottom half, the entire alphabet lined up with corresponding symbols.

"It is a decoder for the Golden Arrows," Arthur told him.

"Grandpa Alistair was a Golden Arrow?"

"Norman, your grandfather Alistair Skylair, was a legend in the Golden Arrows," Arthur said. "Pretty much all of your family was part of the Golden Arrows in one way or another."

"How does it work?" Norman asked turning the decoder over to get a good look at it.

“Well, when the league would send you a message it would just be all of those symbols you see on the side. Of course they would be arranged to form a certain message, or a task of some sort. The message would have a roman numeral somewhere around the edge of the message somewhere. It would be one of the four roman numerals,” Arthur reached out and took the decoder. “Then you would turn the top half like so,” he said as he turned the hemisphere showing Norman, “until the golden arrow pointed at the number. This would change the letters under each symbol, and you would be able to decode the message that was sent to you.”

“Neat,” Norman said, taking the decoder back to look at.

“Of course this is a relic and most people do not communicate by it anymore.”

“Why not?”

“Time changes things Norman.”

“That is too bad,” Norman said, “it is so cool.”

“I will tell you what,” Arthur said, putting his hand on Norman’s shoulder, “I have a decoder myself, maybe after this summer we could communicate to each other through coded messages.”

“I would like that.”

"Come on, Norman, we have to get into the DART." They both got up and made their way into the dive pool room. Norman shoved the decoder into his pocket of his cargo shorts. They climbed down the ladderwell to the door leading into the dive pool. Arthur bent down to enter the room, but Norman stopped in the doorway and watched all the people scurrying around the DART preparing it for launch.

Glitch and Twitch seemed to be in charge, giving commands to all of the elves that carried the blue crystals. The DART was now pointing straight down and the tip was two feet into the water. Norman could see the blue crystals on the top of the DART, they were under some kind of cage.

"How can the crystals fuel the DART?" Norman asked anyone that was listening.

"They are magical, Norman," Meara said to him as she walked up behind him. Norman stepped further into the room, letting her in.

"Magic?"

"Yes, Norman," she told him, "Magic does exist in this world, but humans have forgotten."

"Forgotten what?"

"Forgotten what it was like," she said. "Magic is now reserved for human legends and myths."

Arthur walked over and joined into the conversation, “Magic has been replaced by science, Norman, but the DART is a combination of both magic and science. I call it *modern magic.*” Meara rolled her eyes and walked away. Arthur let out a small laugh.

“Twitch, can we get in now?” Arthur asked.

“Of course.” Twitch reached across the pool with a stick that had a hook at the end. He hooked onto the latch and swung the door open, and then one of the elves laid a metal plank across the gap allowing entry into the DART. Arthur led the way and Norman followed.

When they got into the DART Norman saw that there were three padded seats attached to the walls. Norman climbed into one of the seats and his uncle strapped him in. After he finished, his uncle sat down across from him and strapped in. Glitch popped through the door with two bags in his hands and tossed them into the empty chair.

“Good luck, you two,” Glitch said with a laugh.

“What are those bags for?” Norman asked Arthur.

“We may be gone for a few days.”

“And you may not even come back,” Glitch added.

“Glitch, we don’t need your advice,” Arthur interrupted, “Oh, and Glitch, take good care of my baby while we are gone. Don’t let any pirates take her.”

“You have nothing to worry about; I will take good care of her.”

“You’re kidding, right?” Norman asked. “There is no such thing as pirates.”

“Don’t kid yourself, Norman. Pirates are as real today as they have ever been. Except now they don’t run around with patches on their eyes or parrots on their shoulders. No, they are much more dangerous now. They are armed with machine guns and rocket launchers. They will kill you quickly if they want your ship,” his uncle grimly warned him. Norman took a deep gulp, sorry that he had asked. He watched as Glitch shut the hatch and locked it into place. Norman and his uncle were plunged into darkness.

Chapter Ten

Mordecai Manchild stared out the window at the waves crashing against the coastal rocks and steep cliffs that surrounded his stronghold. He was a tall and foreboding man with black hair peppered with the occasional grey. His chiseled features and large arms resembled an athlete. He was definitely not an athlete. He was a world class criminal overlord and he had his fingers into every type of crime you could imagine. He enjoyed crime and it seemed to fit him well. In his life, crime did pay: he had the finest suits, the largest homes and fastest cars money could buy. Although it wasn't just about money, it was about power.

Dark grey clouds filled the summer sky, keeping the sun from shining. The waters of the ocean became dark and murky blue, resembling a winter storm. A cold breeze was coming in off the water and it brought a chill with it. Even though it was a summer day in Newfoundland, it felt like autumn had already come.

The observation room in which he stood had a wall of floor to ceiling windows that extended halfway around the room, allowing a panoramic view of the peninsula. A balcony wrapped around the entire front of the observation room allowing you to get the same view while outside. On the opposite wall in the room was a bank of monitors keeping Mordecai well informed with current events and business interests.

Many of the monitors were tuned to local, international and financial news networks. Some kept a vigilant watch over the stock markets of the world, and few had live video feeds pertaining to some of his more profitable criminal interests. The last one, well, that was the most important today. It was a live video feed of the two prisons that were housed in the lower levels of this stronghold. Occasionally, he would look back and smile when he saw the two of them.

Mordecai didn't turn when he heard the door open to the observation room. He didn't need to; he already knew that it was James Wolfethorne entering the room. He was waiting for him. James was Mordecai's right hand man. He handled all of the day-to-day operations and all of the security for his boss. Occasionally Mordecai would call on James to do a little dirty work for him and James was all too eager to help.

"We're prepared to run the test," he told Mordecai. James was a lot shorter than his boss, but he was just as muscular. He had brown hair that he kept cropped close to his scalp and brown eyes framed by wire-rimmed glasses. Like his boss, he also dressed very well.

"Perfect, and what of the other one, her cousin?"

"He's in chains in the cell across from her."

"Will she be able to see him from her cell?"

"Of course, sir, she'll be able to. The windows are charged right now, so they're opaque. Once we drop the charges she'll see directly into his cell."

"Good," Mordecai said with a slight grin, "I'll be down shortly and then we can start."

"Yes, sir," James responded and then retreated out of the observation room. He walked down the grey hallway then descended the stairs leading to the lower levels. They were built into the ground and went below the level of the sea. The sides of the stronghold were surrounded by rocks making the lower levels nearly impenetrable.

The Maiden of the Seas sat in the cell with her face pressed against the cool smooth granite of the outer wall. There was one window in the room that was opaque. When the charge was dropped somebody could look in upon her and then recharge the window obscuring her view again. She could feel the waters of the ocean on the outside of the wall.

Her long blue hair with streaks of silver hung in her face. It covered her red, tear stained cheeks. A storm of both anger and sadness raged in her emerald green eyes. Her skin had lost the translucent pearl-like color of the Myhr. She had become sick looking, taking on a grey and spotted look. The dry air in the cell caused her lungs to ache. She needed the moisture in the air of Atlantium. She was slowly dying.

James flipped a switch, causing the window to become instantly clear. The Maiden saw James and Mordecai looking in at her. She flung herself at the window, slamming her palms against it. She glared at them, causing James to feel a little uneasy, but it didn't affect Mordecai at all. They couldn't hear the enraged scream that bellowed from her lungs, but they could see her shake violently.

"Temper, temper, Your Highness," Mordecai said mockingly as he pressed the intercom button. "We wouldn't you want to get hurt or become too tired to help us in our experiment. I need you fully capable for our test."

"I'll do nothing for you," she told him through clenched teeth, "you're an animal."

"Wrong!" he said, a little more menacing this time. "You'll do exactly what I tell you to do, Your Highness!"

"All I want to do is feed you to a shark," she told him.

"And I'm the animal," he said with a little laugh. "I'm sorry but that'll have to wait. You'll participate in our little test and I'll learn how to gain control of the oceans of the world."

"You're right, you're not an animal," she corrected herself. "You're a fool. My powers aren't something you can learn to do. I was born with them and they're part of me; part of my soul."

"I want you to destroy the island of Maui," he said, ignoring her insult.

"Even if I could do that," she said with disgust," I would never do such a thing."

"I believe you will."

Mordecai released the intercom button and turned towards James. She could not hear their conversation, but she saw Mordecai point towards the opaque window across from her cell. Then James pushed a button on the wall releasing the charge to the window and she was able to see in the room.

She immediately fell to her knees and began to sob. In the room was her cousin, Bryan. He was chained to the wall by his arms and additional chains held his legs in place. His body was extremely beaten and bruised. His eyes were swollen shut. Most people would not have been able to recognize him, but his cousin knew the second she saw him. Dried blood encircled his mouth and nose.

"Now, Your Highness, I'll open a connection between you and the sea. And if I don't hear that a tsunami has hit Maui within thirty minutes, you won't see your cousin again," Mordecai instructed her. She stayed kneeling on the floor with her shoulders slumped down. She was coming to the realization that she was powerless to this madman. James turned the switch to allow sea water to start flooding into her room. He stopped it when it reached her thighs, leaving the tube open slightly keeping constant connection between the ocean and the Maiden.

"And, my sweet, the bottom labs are secured from any flooding. So all that will be lost if a tidal wave hits here is my observation room upstairs. It will not even compare to what I can take from you, should that happen." Mordecai turned and walked away to his personal offices down the hall. James walked over and sat down in a chair to wait for his orders to pump the water out of the room. They couldn't leave it in there too long. No telling what could happen if she had that much time in there. She looked up at her cousin in the other room and then closed her eyes. The power started to surge through her body as she opened up to the water. Reaching out through her mind to communicate with the ancient oceans, she felt whole again. The blue birth mark on her shoulder started to glow brightly when the connection was made. Then it all faded as quickly as it came.

Mordecai reclined in his chair with his attention tuned into INN, the International News Network, waiting for the impending doom to be announced. The thought of the destruction that was about to take place didn't really concern him. He was actually more interested in the chip that was placed on her head. He was monitoring the frequencies that occurred when she communicated with the water. He hoped to be able to build a device that would give him control of the water.

“We have some breaking news coming to you now,” the newscaster stated, “Maui was just hit by a tsunami. We don’t have any details as of yet but we will be filling you in as the reports come to us.” A smile crossed Mordecai’s face with the horrible news. He didn’t watch the reporter. He immediately turned to watch the monitoring of her brain activities. He reached over and pressed an intercom button on the wall.

“Pump the water out, James,” he commanded, “then come here.”

“Yes, sir,” James squawked back over the box. It didn’t take long before James was joining him in his office. James stood in front of the desk, knowing full well not to take a seat without his boss’s consent. He knew all too well the fury that his boss was capable of.

“Did we get what we wanted, boss?”

“No, unfortunately it doesn’t look like we can replicate the signals sent from her to the water.”

“What do we do now?” James asked.

“We wait.”

“What are we waiting for, sir?”

“The Myhr are coming and if my sources are correct, so is Arthur Skylair,” an evil smile formed on Mordecai’s face. “Inform all of the guards to prepare for an attack.”

"Do we have a plan?"

Mordecai went over the plan with James. He nodded in agreement with the boss, then stood up and looked out the window towards the inner harbor.

"I don't think we have enough people for the plan," he informed his boss.

"Well, then hire more, as many men as you think it'll take. Then hire some more. I want this to be the end of Arthur Skylair and his righteous beliefs."

Chapter Eleven

Jacob and Elizabeth took a cab from the Edinburgh International Airport. The ride to the headquarters for the Golden Arrows was a scenic one. There are castles scattered throughout the countryside and many of the city landmarks were built before America existed. The small bubble-shaped taxi drove through the large wooden gates of the complex. They were part of the enormous grey stone wall that surrounded the grounds.

It resembled an old fortress with large turrets on each side of the doors and a single turret on each of the six corners of the hexagon shaped wall. The drive led straight to the large castle-like building at the far end of the complex. On either side of the road leading up to it were two similar stone buildings, although not as large as the main structure. These two housed Steinhelm University. Pleasant walking paths connected the three buildings shaded by ancient trees that formed a canopy over the paths.

The cab followed the loop at the end of the drive stopping in front of the massive building. Huge stone steps led up to the front doors. The building resembled a regal building that might have once housed the royal family. The whole place had a surreal and majestic feeling but all that ended when you entered the building.

Jacob paid the driver and slid out of the back seat. He walked around the back of the cab and joined his wife on the other side. They both stood for a second and took in the overpowering sight of the Golden Arrow headquarters.

"I don't like coming to this place," Elizabeth said with a shiver.

"I agree," Jacob said as he put his arm around her shoulder.

"They're not very warm and welcoming here. It is like we are the enemy and they're always on the defensive."

"I know," he agreed, "like they are interrogating you."

The two of them entered the main building, which housed the national war museum of Scotland. It was just a façade. The upper levels were a museum and the top floor was offices for the high council of the League of Golden Arrows. Hidden from the public's view are fourteen underground levels that serve as the hive of Golden Arrow activity.

There are divisions in all of the major cities around the world, but they are lightly staffed. It was here where the majority of the league works and trains. Steinhelm University is the training grounds for future Golden Arrows. The University's true nature was not known by the general public. The public does not apply to the school; the only students that attend must be invited.

Jacob and Elizabeth made their way through the security station at the entrance. They walked across the atrium into the hall of weapons. The walls are covered with exhibits displaying all types of weapons from across the ages. At the end of the hall is a glass display case that covers the wall. Inside the case are medieval weapons such as: swords, maces and crossbows. The battle axes always caught Jacob's attention.

After a few minutes, when the guard monitoring them on the computer confirmed their identity, the glass case separated giving them access to an elevator to the sublevels. They entered the elevator and pressed the button labelled 'C.' There are fourteen buttons on the wall beside the door with three key holes at the bottom of them. Thirteen are labelled from 'A to M' for the corresponding sublevels. There is a single unlit button at the bottom of the panel beneath the three key holes and without the proper keys it will not work. It leads to the dungeons that hold prisoners who have broken treaty laws and laws of magic. Only three people hold the keys and all must be present for it to work.

After leaving the elevator they entered room C-13, basically room 13 on level C. When they walked in, there were already a number of people waiting for them. The two of them glanced at each other prior to taking the chairs across the table from the others. Everyone greeted the couple before starting the meeting.

“Enough with the pleasantries,” Alton Baineswart said raising his voice to be heard, “we must get a move on. We’re already trying to play catch-up with the awful events around the world.”

Alton was a tall, stern-looking Scottish man with orange hair and a bushy mustache to match. He was a member of the senior council. The council was made up of delegates from different countries. Some members also come from different races of mythical and magical beings. The senior cabinet, which oversees the council, is made up of three men; Alton , Norval Needles and Belfour McLeary. Many people believe that Belfour is the true leader of the Golden Arrows and the other two members are merely a formality.

“Jacob,” Alton continued, “we must put this Elven nonsense to rest and behind us quickly. There are other matters that need our attention coming to the forefront.”

“What else is going on?” Jacob asked.

Alton looked down at a small stack of files, opening the top one and then closing it again. He sat there lost in thought, pondering an issue. Alton glanced at his assistant, Carol, sitting next to him. She nodded so slightly that most wouldn’t have noticed.

“The Maiden of the Seas has been kidnapped,” Alton told them.

“What?” Elizabeth said in shock.

"I know," Alton responded, "we are just as concerned."

"Do we know who's responsible?" Jacob asked.

"Our sources have led us to believe that it's Mordecai. We also believe that he had some help from our little friends, the dark elves."

"This is ridiculous!" Elizabeth stated. "What are we doing about this?"

"Nothing officially, but we have made contact with Lord Meryck. We suggested that he contact Arthur for assistance. Since Arthur has firsthand knowledge of Mordecai."

"Are you mad?" she spat out. "My son, Norman, is on the *Sandra Gale* with him right now. He is in no position to assist in such a mission."

"We know," Alton tried to explain, "and we are sorry, but we are unable to take the lead on this right now. We are going to send a ship to aid Arthur but this has to be overseen by someone else right now. Our resources are already over taxed and stretched way too thin. The Blood Elves are attacking humans throughout Germany and Austria, the Goblyn Nation is driving us insane with their shenanigans, there has been a tsunami in the Pacific and some tribe of trolls is wreaking havoc throughout the northern corridor of Canada."

"This is insane!" Jacob said.

"Arthur is our only option right now," Alton persisted, "and possibly the Myhrs' best option."

"Why hasn't a call to arms gone out?" Jacob asked, "Why are we just now hearing of this? There are plenty of sleeper arrows just waiting to be activated. What's going on here?"

"Arthur isn't even with the Golden Arrows anymore. How could you ask him to take part in this?" Elizabeth asked.

"Technically," Carol interrupted, "we didn't ask him to help. Lord Meryck did."

Elizabeth just glared at the assistant. She could have reached across the table and knocked the square, thin rimmed glasses right off her face. Carol just sat there pushing back her bright red curls from her face with an annoying smile on her face.

"Unfortunately, it is what it is," Alton said. "Can we please get back to the business at hand with the elves?"

"Fine," Jacob said, just glad that, if anybody, Norman was with Arthur in this situation. Elizabeth didn't say a word, she just sat there throwing daggers with her eyes at Carol. Alton didn't skip a beat; he knew that both Elizabeth and Jacob were seasoned arrows and they would act accordingly.

"We will assist in sneaking you past patrolling dark and blood elves. You will take the train from Amsterdam to Frankfurt. There we have arranged for a guide to meet you and sneak you into the Elven Kingdom through some old dwarf smuggling mines. After arriving into the Elves' realm you will fall under the protection of the Golden Elves and our treaty with them," Alton told them.

"After the meetings, how do we get out of Europe and back to America?" Jacob asked.

"The Elven dispatch that requested our presence also stated that they will safely escort you home," he told them.

Carol slid an envelope across the table to them. It contained their tickets, passports and some money for the mission. The couple stood to leave and others in the room wished them luck.

Chapter Twelve

The darkness in the DART was disturbing to Norman. He couldn't see his hand in front of his face. Arthur was talking to him, but the direction from which he was talking was undiscernible.

"Uncle Arthur, is it going to be this dark for the entire trip?"

"I don't know, Norman. They have to enchant everything into the blue crystals. And I only insisted that they make sure the communicator was working." And with that, Noah's voice came bellowing over the radio speaker.

"Hello, can you guys hear me?" he asked them.

"We can hear you just fine," Arthur responded. "I hope that you enchanted the light system into the crystals."

"Of course we did, why? Are they not working?"

"No, it is pitch black in here," Norman blurted out.

"Oh, I am sorry," Noah said with a hint of laughter, "let's see if I can help you." There was a slight pause and a clearing of Noah's throat and then he said, "Illuminate!" and a blue light came to life on the ceiling of the DART.

"That's so much better," Norman said with relief, "what happens next?"

"They'll lower us into the water and then release us. The magic from the crystals will take over then and we will whisk off to Atlantium. And beware, it's extremely fast."

The DART started to buck and jolt as it was being lowered into the water. It swayed from side to side until the tip touched into the water. The water somewhat stabilized the motion some.

"We're going to release you now, get ready," Noah warned Arthur.

"We're ready," Arthur told Noah. Norman nodded silently in agreement, but his eyes were a little wider than usual.

"The crystals have been enchanted to take you into the western tunnel. You will arrive at a small outcropping with a beach and the Myhr should be waiting for you. After you get out of the DART just place your hand on the blue crystals and say, 'return.' It will automatically return to us, make sure you have everything out of the DART. It will come back very quickly."

"I understand," Arthur responded. "Get ready Norman."

Norman looked at the strange expression on his uncle's face, it made him a little nervous but it was too late. There was a loud unlatching sound and the DART fell into the water. He could hear the sounds of the water rushing around it. Then the water touched the blue crystals, sending the DART off like a bullet racing towards Atlantium. He could barely make out the words 'safe travels' from Noah as their bodies were crushed into the seats from the g-force.

The DART travelled just ten feet from the side of the mountain that housed Atlantium. The passengers could feel the slight changes in direction as the transport moved to accommodate the ins and outs of the mountainside. The five point restraints held Norman and his uncle in place, but their bags were not so lucky. They were slammed into the ceiling of the DART and the blue light was almost obscured by their bags.

"You were right," Norman shouted to his uncle. "This thing is really moving. It is faster than any roller coaster I have been on."

"This is nothing," Arthur warned him, "wait until it turns into the western cave."

No sooner had he finished talking when the DART started to make a substantial turn into the cave. Norman thought his eyes were going to explode out of his head. The pressure was bordering unbearable. Then both of them were thrown against their harnesses with extreme force. The DART had slammed into a large outcropping of rock from the cavern wall. They could feel that the DART was spiraling out of control. Luckily it was still moving forward like the motion of a perfect football pass.

"Uncle Arthur!" was all that Norman was able to get out.

"Hold onto the handles on the side of your seat," Arthur bellowed back to him.

Norman grabbed onto the u-shaped handles that stuck out from the seat just above his thighs. Only seconds after getting a secure grasp the DART buried its nose into the wall of the cave causing it to flip end over end for over a hundred yards. The crazy ride ended with them slamming into the floor of the cave and sliding thirty feet. The lights flickered on and off, but in the end they remained on.

"Are you okay?" Arthur asked.

"Barely," Norman responded.

"Is everyone okay down there?" Noah squawked over the speaker.

"We're fine!" Arthur said. "What happened?"

"I'm reviewing the images from the sonar sent by the DART and it looks like you hit a large stone or stalactite in the cave. It came up too quick after the turn into the cave for the DART to compensate and maneuver out of the way."

"Can you tell where we are?"

"You're not off course. Unfortunately you still have about three hundred yards to go until it would have surfaced on the beach. Are there any leaks that you can see?"

"No."

"How are we going to get out of here?" Norman asked with fear creeping into his voice.

"Don't worry," Noah told him, "we will figure out what to do. Just sit tight."

Noah covered the microphone with his hand and looked back at Meara. She just looked at the floor and sighed about the situation. She walked over, taking the microphone from Noah so she could speak to Arthur and Norman.

"Arthur," Meara's voice came over the intercom, "I believe that the crystals were knocked loose during the crash. Otherwise the DART would still be moving towards its destination."

"What do we have to do to get this thing moving again?" Arthur asked.

"There is nothing you can do," she told him. "You would have to get out and reset the crystals. Unfortunately the water pressure would crush you."

"So what can we do then?" Norman added a little more frantic than his uncle.

“I am going to contact Lord Meryck through the waterlink and see if he could send some Myhr to your aid.”

“Please hurry,” Arthur insisted, “it may not be leaking but we’ll eventually run out of air.”

“I understand,” Meara said and then left to go use the waterlink.

Arthur felt some warm liquid on his face. He looked around for some kind of leak or even a ruptured pipe. There wasn’t anything wrong, everything was intact. He rubbed the liquid away only to see blood on his hand. Only then did he realize the pain shooting through his head.

“Is everything okay?” Norman asked.

“I’m fine,” Arthur said, shaking the darkness that was creeping into his vision away.

Chapter Thirteen

Norval Needles, a high council member of the League of Golden Arrows, sat in his private office in the headquarters top floor. He picked up the brown handset of his old-fashioned corded phone and punched in a number. The phone rang four times before being answered.

"Hello," a raspy woman's voice said.

"Hello," Norval responded.

"You should not have called," she told him.

"Jacob and Elizabeth left earlier this morning," he responded. "They are heading to Germany where they'll meet the guide you have supplied."

"Good," she said in a more pleasant tone, "Fayne wishes to speak with you."

Norval waited on a silent phone for the leader of the dark elves to pick up the phone. He wiped the beads of sweat from his forehead and ran his hand through the black curly mane on top of his head. His hand returned to drumming his fingers on the large mahogany desk top.

"It's good to hear from you my good friend, Norval," Fayne said, bordering on sarcasm.

"We are not friends," Norval said, "and we shouldn't be using names."

"Don't be a coward. I will not hide from your childish and pathetic organization. In a few years they will be no more."

"Enough," Norval said, annoyed. "I have done what you asked, now release the funds."

"Oh, we're not done yet, councilman."

"We had a deal!"

"I know, Norval, but you need to complete your side of the deal."

"What else do you need from me," Norval sighed, resigned to the fact that he would still be involved with this monster.

"You will travel to America and meet me in Boston. You're to bring the Blood Ring from your archives with you."

"Are you crazy? Do you think that I can just waltz out with a magical artifact like that?"

"I'm far from crazy and besides, if anyone asks, you can just tell them you are returning it to the rightful owners. The League of Golden Arrows took it from my ancestors," Fayne insisted.

"What's going to happen to Elizabeth and Jacob?"

"Leave them to me," Fayne told him, "you just make your way to America! I will take care of them."

Norval slammed the phone into the cradle. Soon after, Carol lightly knocked then entered without waiting for a reply. She held his coat and a packed overnight bag. He looked at her over his black rimmed glasses.

"You were listening," he asked her.

"Will you be leaving immediately?" she asked.

"Yes, I must figure out how to get the ring and then I will leave," he told her. "I shall return as soon as possible."

"Is there anything you need me to do while you are gone?"

"Just be my eyes and ears. There are dark times ahead of us and we'll need to stay ahead of the chaos."

"I will."

"Thank you," he said, taking his bag and coat and departing for America.

Chapter Fourteen

Jacob and Elizabeth arrived in Frankfurt, Germany early in the morning. They were supposed to travel straight through to Heidelberg, but changed course after receiving a message from the Golden Elves. They sat in a small coffee and pastry shop just around the corner from the train station. After about fifteen minutes a thick little hairy dwarf came waddling into the store. In most cases this would have alarmed some people, but this store was owned by a member of the League of Golden Arrows.

He climbed into a chair at their table. After glancing over both of his shoulders, Günter Grendlehook settled into his chair.

"The Golden Elves have contacted me and asked that I take you to their realm for an important meeting," Günter told them.

"We also received a letter at our hotel, in Amsterdam, suggesting that we meet with you to arrange secret passage through the tunnels," Jacob confirmed

"What's going on?" Elizabeth interrupted. "We were supposed to meet with Durin and he was going to be our guide."

"Durin was captured by the Dark Elves, and then he was conveniently released to be your guide. It was probably a trap but you can go with him if you like," Günter said with an awkward smile. "It makes no difference to me, I'm just in it for the gold."

"No, it's fine," Jacob resigned. "We'll be glad to use your services. When do we leave?"

"Do you have the gold?"

"Of course."

"Then we'll leave first thing in the morning," Günter said. "Take the train leaving at eight-thirty for Heidelberg, I will meet you there."

"Tomorrow!" Elizabeth intervened. "We can't be late for the hearings with the elves."

"You will not be late," Günter said, eyeing her. "I have to meet with a client and get an item from him. Since we're heading to Heidelberg I might as well make some extra gold on this trip."

"We better make it on time," she threatened.

"You will," he grunted. "I know all of the shortcuts through the mountain. You'll do far better with me then you could ever have done with Durin, you'll see."

Günter finished the last of that sentence as he removed himself from the table and left the coffee shop, leaving Norman's parents to sit and ponder the situation. After some small talk about the changes and latest events, they retired to an inn just up the block.

The following morning Norman's parents sat on a train racing towards Heidelberg. Jacob stretched out across the seat in their cabin and stared out the window at the majestic scenery as it moved past them. Elizabeth was engrossed in a novel she grabbed off a book cart that they passed in the dining car. The view from the window was breathtaking and Jacob couldn't get enough of it, he secretly wished to move to Germany. He was sliding his foot over, trying to knock the book down. She would just push his foot off and never move her eyes from the book.

Just then there was a loud rapping at the door to their cabin. They looked at each other and just shrugged. All they could see through the smoked glass was the shadow of someone tall.

"Can we help you with something?" Jacob called out. There wasn't a response from the person. The rapping came again and this time a little louder than the last. Elizabeth looked at Jacob with concern in her eyes. Jacob got up cautiously and slid open the door. His shoulders relaxed when he saw Adelwyn, a golden elf of the ruling family, standing in his doorway. The Golden Elves were regal looking. All of them were tall and thin, their hair was golden blonde and their skin was somewhere between white and tan. They held their heads high no matter what the circumstances.

"Adelwyn," he said in surprise, "why didn't you respond when we called out?"

"I didn't hear you," Adelwyn said, "the train is loud. May I come in?"

"Of course you can," Elizabeth said as she stood up to greet the new guest. "It's great to see you again," she said, hugging him. Even though it was not customary in the Elven society to hug, he knew this family well, so returned the embrace.

"I'm sorry to say it this way," Jacob cut in, "but why are you here? I didn't think that we would have seen you prior to arriving in your realm."

"I know, but times have changed and things are much more dangerous now. Father thought it would be safer if I traveled with you as added security."

Adelwyn's father, Ederwyn Elflunger, is the steward for the realm of the Golden Elves. All of the royal family, except a young princess, were assassinated in the last elven war. Since then, she has been in hiding. When she reaches the age of five hundred years she will take her place as the rightful ruler of the Golden Elves, until that time the Elflunger family is overseeing things.

There are many who believe that this is the reason for all of the upheaval in the realms. She will be of the age to assume the throne in one year. In order to keep her safe, even the ruling family doesn't know of her whereabouts.

"What do you mean things aren't safe?" Elizabeth asked.

"There have been three more attacks on humans since the last time my father talked with the high council," Adelwyn informed her.

"Where is this happening?" she asked.

"Here, in the Black Forest. Things have escalated rather quickly and that is why Arion has decided to call the hearing in the great hall."

"Who is Arion?" Jacob asked.

"He has been chosen by the trees to be the speaker of the clans. All of the elven clans; dark, light and neutral have approved his position. At least we agree on something now and then."

"Much has changed since our last visit," Elizabeth said. "What happened to the old speaker?"

"She was murdered by blood elves," Adelwyn told them. "Of course, there is no proof of this and my father would be upset at me for just suggesting it, but that is what I believe. The Dark Elves were very fast to confirm the new appointment of Arion."

"I thought you said that the trees appointed him?" Jacob asked.

“I did and that is the only reason that the elves of light have agreed to confirm him. I believe, though, that the Dark Elves are behind him, trying to manipulate their way into the throne room,” suggested Adelwyn.

“You will make a formidable general in her majesty’s forces when the princess returns,” Elizabeth said with a smile bright enough to light the darkness.

“Thank you,” he said, returning the smile.

“Please,” Jacob interjected, “tell me of the new attacks in the forest.”

“They were very brutal and we found traces of dark glimmer magic in the areas of the attacks. The glimmer magic can mean only one thing. A dark elf must have been trying to cover his tracks. I can only hope that the dark elves will have to answer for this chaos at the Great Hall.”

“What happened to the people that were attacked?” Elizabeth pushed for more information.

“They didn’t make it, unfortunately,” he told her grimly. “I am truly sorry, Elizabeth.”

“How is your father handling all of this?” Jacob asked. “It must be difficult, as steward he is responsible for the peace in the Black Forest and your realms.”

"He is overwhelmed and it is easily noticeable. The heads of all the families are putting a lot of pressure on him to squash this before it turns to all-out war. Our family's guard is constantly scouring the forest looking for traces of blood elves. The once beautiful city of Favelyn has fallen into darkness. Elves don't leave their houses at night and the fires are kept burning long into the night to ward away the darkness."

"That is terrible," Elizabeth told him.

"It is," Adelwyn agreed.

Chapter Fifteen

Being trapped in the DART was starting to feel like a nightmare to Norman. The lights were flickering more often. His uncle looked like he was seriously injured. He kept falling in and out of sleep. It seemed to take days before Meara came back on the radio.

"Are you two all right?" she asked them.

"I don't know," Norman said with concern in his voice. "My uncle is sleeping and it is very hard to wake him up. I think he is hurt bad."

"Okay, Norman," she said in a soothing voice, "I have contacted the Myhr and they are coming for you right now."

"How long will it take?"

"It shouldn't take too long. They have already left Atlantium and you are not that far from the beach in their cave."

"UNCLE ARTHUR!" Norman yelled. "He isn't waking up!"

"Don't worry, Norman," she assured him, "the Myhr will be there shortly; they'll make it in time, I promise."

Just then the DART jolted forward and rocked side to side. It felt like someone was trying to wiggle it free. It took a moment but the submersible was pulled free from the cave floor. It was being dragged across the ground.

“Alright!” Norman shouted in delight, “they are here and we are being pulled to shore.”

“What is happening?” Meara asked with concern in her voice. It was far too soon for the Myhr to have arrived. Meara had just left the waterlink, where she was talking to them and asking them to go to Norman’s aid. Something else was responsible for releasing the DART and she was worried.

“Norman, you are sure about being dragged and not just sliding?” she asked.

“Yes, I am sure. I know that we aren’t sliding because we’re going uphill.”

“Norman, something other than the Myhr is dragging you out of the water.”

“How could you know that?”

“It’s too soon,” she warned him, “they wouldn’t have made it there yet.”

“Who do you think it is?” Norman cried out rapidly.

"I don't know," she said, "be careful!"

Norman suddenly felt a wave of fear and nausea flood over him. There was no way of knowing what thing was out there pulling on the DART. It could be some crazy monster that his uncle hadn't told him about yet, maybe it thought the DART was some kind of food, like a clam or something like that. He was starting to make himself more scared with every thought. It wouldn't take it long to break open this shell to get the tasty morsel inside. Norman just sat there with his eyes closed fearing the worst.

The DART stopped moving. Then he felt it shake once more and then get hoisted out of the water. The sound of water streaming down the transport and back into the sea could be heard through the walls. They were launched into the air, spinning once again and crashed down into the ground. Norman had no clue where he was and now he ached all over. How the DART landed left him dangling from his chair, held in place by his harness. The door to the DART was ripped right off the hinges in the crash. He unlocked the straps and fell out of his seat, just missing his uncle.

"Uncle Arthur, are you okay?" he asked lightly shaking his uncle. Arthur stirred a little but still didn't wake up. He heard some noises coming from the outside of the DART. Wondering what to do, he decided to take a quick look outside and see where he was. The cavern was very dark and it was hard to see anything. There was some light coming from vein-like tubes running across the ceiling of the cave. They radiated a dull yellowish orange colored light.

"I'll be right back," he said to his uncle as he lifted himself up and out of the DART.

His eyes started to become a little more accustomed to the darkness, but he still couldn't see anything. He was wondering what lifted them out of the water or what was making that noise as he slid off the side. When he turned around, away from the DART, Norman fell backwards onto the ground, trying to back pedal as quick as possible. There in front of him stood an enormous creature. The bottom half of it resembled a crab, the large blue shell was moving across the cavern floor on six small muscular legs. The top half, on the other hand, was more like a human. Except his left arm, which looked like a large blue crab pincer. Norman was terrified.

"Don't hurt me," Norman pleaded as he scrambled backwards.

"He will not hurt you," a voice said from the darkness. Norman's head spun towards it.

"Who's there?" Norman asked into the darkness.

"I am Michael."

Norman watched as a pale white man came walking out of the shadows with tan cotton pants that stopped just below his calves. He looked like a man at first until you took a better look at him. The entire back half of him was a hard shell that molded perfectly with his body. It was a dull light grey blue color and resembled the shell of the other creature.

"We didn't mean to scare you," Michael told him, raising his hands in a peaceful gesture.

"Did you pull the DART out of the water?" he asked them glancing towards the vehicle.

"Yes"

"How did you find us?"

"It was just being in the right place at the right time. You actually slammed into the cave floor not too far from one of our cavern entrances."

Norman and Michael both looked over at some oncoming lights at the same time. They were coming quickly towards them. Michael looked down at Norman and frowned.

"That would be the Myhr coming for you," Michael told him.

"From Atlantium?" Norman asked.

"Yes, and unfortunately they will not take kindly to us being here. What is your name, little one?"

"My name is Norman, but my family calls me Normal Norman."

“Well Normal Norman, I am sure we’ll meet again someday,” Michael stated. Then he turned towards the large creature with him, “Mullick, we must go now.” Then they both turned and dashed into the water, disappearing beneath the surface.

Chapter Sixteen

When the guards reached him, Michael and Mullick had already disappeared into the water. There were five of them; two went to Norman and two more tended to the smashed up DART, helping Arthur out of it. The last of them ran and dove straight into the water with what looked like a long spear.

The Myhr looked similar to Michael minus the hard shell on the back. They were very pale with nearly translucent skin. Two of them helped Norman stand and brushed him off. They looked him over for injuries. Their eyes sat more on the side of a thin and narrow head. On both sides of the ribs were gills. Norman noticed that they had fingers and toes like him, except they had thin webbing connecting them.

"Are you okay?" one of them asked Norman.

"I'm fine, thank you," Norman said, slightly hesitating. "Are you Myhr?"

"Yes, we are."

Norman watched as the other two gently pulled Arthur out of the DART. They laid him down in the sand next to it, cradling his head in one's lap. The other Myhr pulled out an old looking glass tube with a wooden cork. The liquid inside was a dark royal blue and radiated magic. They squeezed his face with one hand, making his lips part open.

"What are you doing?" Norman asked, going to his uncle. One of the Myhr guards grabbed his arm, keeping him back.

"He is helping him," the guard said to Norman, "he has a bad injury and needs our help."

"What is that stuff?" Norman asked.

"It is an elixir of life from the Matron of the Seas. It will heal his wounds," the guard said.

Norman looked at the guard in amazement and then at his uncle. The guard holding his uncle poured the elixir into Arthur's mouth. He responded and swallowed it down. It worked quickly; his uncle started to moan and stir. Shortly after drinking the elixir he sat up, holding his head. Norman ran over to him and knelt down beside him.

"Uncle Arthur, are you okay?"

"I'll be fine," he told Norman, "but I'm sure glad they got here quickly."

Everyone turned and looked at the water as the Myhr came back out. He shook his head and looked back at the water. He still carried the long spear and walked straight at Arthur.

“Ah Coulter, there you are,” Arthur said with a smile.

“Hello Arthur, it is good to see you, my friend.”

“And you as well.”

“You seemed to have trouble on your trip in.”

“Yes we did,” Arthur confirmed, “and what is going on here?”

“When we were coming down the cave there were some Crusteans surrounding this young man. They took off into the water when we got closer and have gotten away.”

“This young man is Norman,” he said doing the introductions. “He is Jacob and Elizabeth’s son.”

“Well then, it is an honor to meet you, young Norman. I am Coulter, the captain of the royal guard.”

“Captain?” Arthur asked, surprised.

“Unfortunately we lost many in the kidnapping. The soldiers detonated explosives, caving in the eastern passage on our heads. It is still an honor to be offered this position.”

“What are Crusteans?” Norman asked.

“They’re monsters, Norman, and you’re lucky that they didn’t rip your limbs off.”

Norman remained silent, he thought back to his encounter and remembered that they didn't seem to be violent. The one named Michael was nice to him. Everyone helped gather all of the gear from the DART.

"We must go," Coulter said, starting to walk away. "Crusteans frighten easy but they'll be back and in greater numbers."

"What about the DART?" Norman asked.

"Just leave it here," he told him, "we will send a team to return it to the *Sandra Gale* eventually."

Everyone fell in behind Coulter and Arthur as they made their way down the tunnel. Norman walked in silence for a little bit, deep in his own thoughts. Every now and then he would look back at the water, until it was lost in the darkness.

The team of royal guards led Arthur and Norman through a series of tunnels leading deep into the earth. Norman had no clue where they were by now, but then again he didn't care too much. The walls of the tunnel were glistening with water and they had some kind of mold-like substance growing on them. The tunnels were enormous. The ceiling reached thirty feet up and the tunnel stretched twenty feet wide. It was very cold and there was very little light. There were tubes that ran the length of the tunnel that had a light glow coming from them. They resembled roots or veins running along the wall. They were definitely not in a straight line.

“What are those tubes with light in them?” he asked Arthur.

“Light veins. They are resin tubes. They fill them with special plankton from the bottom of the ocean. They actually let off their own light,” Arthur told him.

“What is plankton?”

“They are microscopic organisms that live in the water, kind of like micro-fish.”

“Are the guards taking us to Atlantium right now or somewhere else?”

“We are indeed taking you to Atlantium,” the guard behind Norman answered him. The guard’s voice had a rough tone to it.

“We’ve been expecting Arthur’s arrival. You are somewhat of a surprise but a welcome surprise nonetheless,” the guard continued. The group continued in silence. It was driving Norman crazy, even though there was some light, it was still pretty dark in there.

“Tell me about the kidnapping,” Arthur asked.

“It happened ten days ago. A stealthy team of murderers, if you ask me, came in through Lake Knorr. They moved quietly and quickly through the streets to the Maiden’s house. They knew exactly where they were going. When they reached the house they took her with great force. They were armed very well. In pursuit of them we lost many guard members including the captain. The Maiden’s family lost a few members of their personal guard. They haven't been able to find their nephew Bryan yet either. We believe that he was abducted as well. We fear the worst for him, because he has nothing that would make him useful to his captors."

"Except to be used as leverage against his cousin, the Maiden," Arthur filled in.

"Exactly, that is why we must move quickly. Out of the two his life is in the greatest danger right now."

"Have you discovered who is behind this yet?" Arthur asked.

"We have. It is Mordecai." Coulter informed him.

"Are you sure?"

"We received information from our informant network about Mordecai's involvement, but it was then confirmed by our own spies and guards."

The conversation was brought to a halt when they came around a bend in the tunnel. There was a brilliant light coming from the opening at the end of the tunnel. Norman paused for a moment.

"Is that Atlantium?" Norman asked.

"Yes, it is," the guard answered him. The entrance to the city looked like a mouth opened to let them out. Pointed stones hung from the ceiling and came out of the ground forming what seemed to be a set of teeth. They all had to navigate their way through them to get into the city. As Norman walked through the opening his eyes were temporarily blinded by the light. Once his eyes refocused, his heart jumped with excitement. In front of him sat an underwater city, Atlantium, and it was awesome.

Chapter Seventeen

Norman stood on a ledge overlooking the city of Atlantium. It was enormous. There were three large lakes; two were connected by a large river that separated what seemed to be a palace from the rest of the city. Then a long, thin stream connected the river to the last lake on the other side of this massive cave. The wooden stairs that led down from the ledge that they stood on would put them directly into the part of the city with all of the little buildings.

"What are all of those little buildings down there?" Norman asked Coulter.

"Those are houses, Norman, this is where all of the Myhr live," he answered him.

"Sweet," Norman said.

"Do you see all of those large buildings surrounding the large lake in the back?"

"I do," Norman answered, "what are they?"

"Those are aquaculture buildings, basically they are fish farms."

"This place is so cool," Norman said with amazement.

“I am sorry to break up this school session,” Arthur cut in, “but we must get to the palace and meet with Lord Meryck.”

“I apologize, you’re absolutely right. I’m just proud of my city.”

“Don’t worry about it. We must be going,” Arthur said as he started to make his way down the old wooden stairs. The stairs ended in the residential section of the city and all the Myhr that were walking around in the streets immediately stopped and looked at them. This didn’t halt Arthur’s stride one bit; he continued to make his way across streets towards the palace. Norman took this opportunity to ask some more questions.

“I saw a river separating the palace from the rest of the city, how are we going to get there?” he asked Coulter.

“There are two wooden suspension bridges that were made from old ships that sunk long ago. It hangs about twenty feet above the river. We will cross there.”

“Twenty feet,” Norman said, “That’s not too high. Has anyone fallen before?”

“Some,” Coulter told him as they walked. Norman was just looking around staring at all of the cool sights as they continued on. Finally they reached the bridge spanning across the river. Norman looked to his left and saw the most beautiful waterfall he had ever seen. It must have been hundreds of feet wide, and it poured down out of the ceiling of the cave, hiding the wall on the far side of Lake Knorr.

"That's one big waterfall," Norman pointed out.

"It's the home of the Matron of the Seas," Coulter told Norman.

"Who's that?"

"She's the keeper of all of the water in the oceans."

"What do you mean the keeper?"

"She can control it and she can communicate with it. She is very powerful." Coulter guided Norman towards the entrance of the bridge. The group slowly made their way across the old creaky bridge. As they reached the opposite side he saw the palace of the royal family. It was built into the side of the cave. Parts of it were made from large stalactites coming from the roof of the cave, and they were as big as large buildings from his hometown. The main portion came out of the rock with a huge staircase leading to the thirty-foot high doors that led into the palace. There were two huge stalagmites that stood on both sides of the stairs that were formed and carved into watch towers.

"Cool!" Norman said.

Norman and Arthur were shown to their separate rooms in the palace. He felt a little weird to be staying by himself in the palace of a race of people that lived under the water. "*This is not normal*!" he thought to himself. Then he saw the huge glass doors that led to a balcony overlooking the city of Atlantium.

Norman stood there for a long time just taking in the sights of the city. He could see the three lakes and all the buildings. All this was neat, but it was the huge waterfall that his eyes always went back to. He wondered what the Matron behind it looked like. It was then that Norman realized just how tired he was, so he stretched out on a lounge chair on the balcony. He didn't want to sleep in the big room by himself. Shortly after putting his head on the cushion, he fell into a deep sleep.

***

He was awakened suddenly by a young Myhr girl shaking his shoulders. He sat straight up in surprise and smacked his forehead against hers. He fell off the lounge chair holding his head and the girl fell backwards holding her own head.

"What are you doing?" he shouted.

"Ouch," she responded, "keep your voice down; you are going to wake all of Atlantium."

Norman opened his eyes, realizing suddenly that it was dark in the city. All of the buildings that had lights on just earlier were now dark. He continued to rub his head and looked over at the girl. She was a Myhr with long blue hair; her skin was almost bright white.

"Who are you?"

"I'm Penelope, the keeper of the Matron, like an assistant to her. She has sent me to bring you to her chamber."

"What?"

"The Matron wants to speak with you; she seems very excited that you're here."

"How does she know me?'

"I don't know, but she doesn't regularly seek out people besides Lord Meryck. Actually, since the birth of the Maiden, only the lord and I have been in there, and that was over fourteen years ago."

"What does she want?"

"She didn't say, but it must be important. Come on we have to go," she said as she helped him up. They both made their way into the bedroom and to the door. She opened it and looked around for the guards. She led Norman out and down the hall to the base of a large statue of Lord Meryck. She went behind it and pushed a secret lever under the ledge that wrapped around the base of the statue. A door swung open leading to a staircase. There was a lantern hanging just inside. She grabbed it and entered onto the stairs. Norman followed her reluctantly. The door slid closed behind him as he passed completely into the passage.

"Is this the only way into the Matron's chamber?"

"No, this will actually let us out just behind the guards that protect the piers with the boat."

"Do you usually have to sneak into her chamber?"

"No, I don't," she told him, "but you do."

"Oh," Norman said, "why?"

"Just like I told you, nobody enters that place."

The walk through the tunnel didn't take too long. They went down pretty far then walked some more, eventually going up a short set of stairs leading to a wall. She pulled a lever down and it swung open. She stepped out and quietly made her way down the pier towards a small wooden row-boat tied to the end. Norman followed after her. Glancing over his shoulder, he saw a group of guards that could barely be seen in the torch light. They climbed down a ladder and into an old wooden boat.

"Get down in the bottom of the boat," she said, "between the seats and crouch down. They expect to see me coming and going, but not with someone else in the boat."

"Okay," Norman said as he slid down low enough so he could just see above the edge of the boat and where they were going. Penelope untied the boat and pushed off using one of the oars. She then took the other oar and started rowing to the other side of the lake. As they got closer Norman could make out another pier sticking out from the wall next to the waterfall. Just to the right of the pier, about fifty yards away, he saw a small area of shoreline sticking out with about twenty or so torches lighting it up very well. Where the land met the wall was an opening to a cave that was enclosed with large metal bars, like a prison.

"What's that place over there?" Norman asked, gesturing towards the cave.

"It's the entrance to the realm of the Crusteans."

"Are the Crusteans monsters?"

"They're mutations, actually. They were formed by some Myhr scientist. They took volunteers from the army and guards. Promising to make them strong and nearly invincible with the strong shells, they merged the genes of crustaceans with Myhr. What a mistake that was. It started with ten or so. At first it seemed to work, but after they altered about a hundred they began to see some alterations in the people. A war broke out in the middle of the city. The Crusteans were violent and mindless, unable to even communicate. They just attacked. The royal guard fought them and pushed them back into that cave. The dwarves built us that gate. It is said that only a dragon could break through it."

When the story was finished both she and Norman just sat for a second and stared at the gate that led into the realm. It was pitch black behind the bars. Norman thought of Michael at that moment.

"You said that they couldn't communicate?" he asked her.

"That's right."

"I talked to one in the cave, before the guards arrived."

"That's impossible," she said as the boat came up to the pier at the base of the waterfall. She tied it off again, and then climbed up the ladder. Norman pulled himself up and then grabbed onto the ladder and followed her.

"They were never able to speak before," she told him.

"That's the funny thing about mutations," Norman said as he got to the top of the ladder and pulled himself up to the pier, "they continue to mutate." She looked at Norman and then looked over towards the cave.

"We have to hurry, the Matron's waiting." She made her way down the pier. It ended at a very old and dangerous set of stone stairs leading up and behind the waterfalls. Norman stood there for a second and looked up the stairs.

"Of course there wouldn't be any railings. That would be just too normal."

"There has never been any railing on these stairs, it's a defense. Stay close to the wall and away from the edge; unless you would like to take a dip in the lake."

They both walked up the stairs with their backs against the wall. As they got closer to the top of the stone stairs the mist from the waterfall made it slick. Norman caught himself slipping a couple of times. It took a while to get to the top because they were moving very slowly up the stairs. They started to walk behind the waterfall, Norman's heart pounded as he took his first step behind it.

"It's just like some of the stories I've read," he yelled to be heard over the roar of the falls.

"What is?" she asked him.

"People living behind waterfalls," he yelled back, "I half expect Sir Lancelot to step out any minute now."

"Who's Sir Lancelot?"

"Lancelot, he's a knight of the round table," he told her. She looked back at him and just shrugged her shoulders and kept walking forward. Eventually they came to a large opening in the wall. It was lined with torches. It went about fifty feet into the mountain then dropped down out of sight. She started walking in but stopped about fifteen feet in front of a nice wooden door.

"Is this it?" he asked.

"No, this is where I live. You must continue on by yourself. The Matron is waiting for you; she's at the bottom of the cave."

"The bottom of the cave?"

“Yes,” was all she said as she disappeared into the room behind the wooden door.

Norman slowly walked towards the back of the cave. When he got to the end he realized why he couldn’t see where the cave went. It was a ledge and he could make out some light about thirty feet down. About two feet from the edge there was a rope connected to a beam of wood that spanned the width of the cave and was buried into the wall on either end. “Well, here goes nothing,” he said to the darkness. Reaching out, he grabbed the rope and slowly lowered himself down.

Chapter Eighteen

Norman walked into the Matron's chamber. He gazed upon the walls and ceiling with awe. The walls were covered with beautiful carvings telling stories of the lives of the Myhr. His eyes travelled the length of the wall seeing wrought iron sconces holding torches. He could hear water dripping from the ceilings and feel the moisture in the air. There were three rooms that he could see; each separated by an archway leading into the next room. Shimmering blue tapestries hung lavishly around the room. The only other source of light came from the pool that ran into all three rooms through the archway.

The water had a blue green light illuminating from it. It gave the room an eerie look as the light danced with the ripple of the water. Norman stopped in the middle of the first room at the edge of the pool. He looked into the pool and could see the bottom as if he could reach down and touch it by only reaching his hand into it. Little did he know but the bottom of the pool was actually two feet down, the clarity of the water just gave the illusion of a very shallow pool. The bed of the pool was covered with artifacts, coins, jewelry, and different pieces of art. While Norman was gazing at the bottom of the pool, the Matron entered into the room from one of the connecting chambers.

“I’m so glad to finally meet you, Norman,” the Matron said. Her voice sounded like a song. Norman almost lost his footing when she called out to him.

“I’m so sorry, ma’am,” Norman barely got the words out of his mouth.

“It’s nothing to worry about, my child. Please come into the pool with me. I’ve a lot to show you and time is something that we cannot spare,” she said, waving him into the pool. Norman slowly climbed down into the pool. He was surprised to find out that the pool was deeper than he thought. The water was very cold, but his body quickly got used to the temperature change. When Norman got closer to the Matron he noticed that her skin had a blue green hue to it and her eyes, he could see the oceans in her eyes. The Matron reached her hand out and took Norman’s hand. Her skin was cold and moist to the touch.

“Penelope said that you wanted to see me.”

“I did, Norman. I would like to talk to you about the rescue of the Maiden.”

“What can I do? I am just a normal kid!”

“You’ve no idea how far you are from normal, Norman. How many kids do you know that spend their summer under the ocean talking to a woman that can control water?”

"None, I guess."

"Come with me, Norman," she said and led him into the back room of the chamber. He followed her into the room. It was lit by torches and the walls were covered with old blue tiles. She pointed to the water and Norman looked, but didn't see anything. She leaned forward and started to run her finger through the water in a circular motion. Nothing was there at first, but then Norman started to see some images of buildings in ruins coming into view.

"What's this place?"

"Mordecai has already forced the Maiden to destroy an island called Maui in the Pacific Ocean. We must move quickly before more damage can be done."

"What do you want me to do?"

She moved her finger around in the opposite direction and the image of the island vanished while another picture started to take form. Norman tried to figure out what it was. It was a building on a rocky bluff overlooking the ocean.

"Is this the place where they're keeping the Maiden?"

"You see, Norman? You're very capable of undertaking the mission I have for you."

"I don't understand, what do you mean a mission for me?"

She leaned forward and grabbed Norman's hand. He felt the cold wetness of her touch again. This time it was different though. She closed her eyes and he started to feel some warmth surging from her. It started in his wrist but then it started to fill his body with a tingling heat. When she released him, he fell back into the water, sinking underneath it. He opened his eyes and saw the Matron reaching down towards him. She grabbed onto him and pulled him out of the water.

"Norman, are you okay?"

"Yes, yes, I think I am," he told her. "What was that?"

"In a couple of months I would transfer power to her, so that she could take over as the Matron of the Seas. I've given you the power that I was to transfer to her. All you have to do is touch the birthmark on her right shoulder and the power will flow from you to her."

"What kind of birthmark?"

"It will look like an upside down drop of water with three drops of water around it. They are dark blue with a tint of grey," she pulled the right shoulder of her gown down a couple of inches, showing him the birthmark. "We all have it Norman. Every Maiden is born with it. It allows us to know who'll take over as the Matron."

"Why me?"

"What do you mean?"

"Why have you selected me to do this job?"

"Your heart is pure. It's filled with innocence. Others would be corrupted by the power."

Norman shook his head. "I don't get it," he told her.

"You will in time, trust me," she smiled at Norman. "We're done now. You must go now and if you leave out that way," she pointed in the direction opposite from where he entered, "it'll be a shortcut."

Norman thanked her and turned to leave. As he got closer to the other side he couldn't see a door. It didn't matter though; this place seemed to be full of secret passages. So he continued forward, not paying attention to where he stepped. When he walked into the area of darker water it was too late, he was already sinking into the water before he realized what was happening.

He sank under the water and was propelled downward by a strong current. It was dark, but he could see through the water easily. It was some kind of tunnel. He started to get a little freaked out. "*What if I run out of air?*" he thought. Then he saw all the eyes looking at him as he raced through the water. He moved past them too quickly before he could see what they were. Just then, Norman splashed out of the water and fell to the ground some ten feet below. He laid there hurting. Checking his bumps and bruises, he peered up at the hole in the ceiling that he dropped from.

"How's that?" he asked himself out loud, but before he could answer, a large claw slammed down around his neck and scooped him up. He grabbed onto the claw, which helped relieve some of the pressure off his neck. It was a Crustean similar to the one he'd met in the tunnel, but he could tell this was different. Norman could feel the claw starting to squeeze around his neck, then darkness started to engulf him.

Chapter Nineteen

Norman woke up in a damp cave surrounded by the Crusteans. There were hundreds of them. He thought he was in some kind of dream or nightmare. He slowly stood up and looked around, the Crusteans were all different. They were all mutated in their own way. Some just had claws for one or both hands, while others were mostly crustacean and less human.

"Hello, Norman," Michael said, walking up from behind. Norman spun around to see him and a woman walking up next to him. She looked identical to him with the exception of being a female and the hard shell back had some additional hues of red with the blues.

"Hello," Norman responded.

"I apologize for the neck thing," Michael told him.

"What's this place?" Norman asked rubbing his neck.

"This is our home, Norman. Ever since our kin, the Myhr, exiled us from Atlantium, we have lived down here. We call it the realm underneath."

"Really, that's terrible."

"It isn't so bad and besides it is our home now."

"Sorry, I didn't mean any offense."

"None taken," Michael said with a dismissive wave of his hand. Until now the female had remained quiet. She stepped past Michael to stand in front of Norman. Her eyes were blue-grey and felt like they could burn right through Norman.

"Forgive my brother," she says with a glare back at her brother. "He doesn't see the danger in anything. The real question is why are you here, Norman?"

"I don't know, one second I was in the Matron's chamber and the next I was splashing out of some water landing in your cave."

"That's not what I meant, why are you in Atlantium? You are not Myhr, so obviously you are a guest of theirs."

"My uncle and I came to help them."

"That's what I thought," she said with an evil grin and then she nodded to someone behind Norman. Once again Norman felt the ever so familiar pinch of claws grabbing his neck, this time it forced him to his knees. Michael pushed pass his sister.

"What are you doing? Ulrich, release him this instant!" he told the Crustean guard behind Norman. The guard refused, he looked between Michael and his sister, Crystal.

"You'll do no such thing," she scowled at Ulrich, then Crystal turned facing the rest of the Crusteans surrounding them, "My fellow citizens of the realm, the Myhr seemed to have developed a plan to attempt to finally rid themselves of us. They have even started to recruit help from this race of humans. Our spies inform us that they are preparing for some kind of battle."

"No," Norman struggled to get it out.

"Silence," she spat out, crouching into Norman's face, "do not try and fill our heads with your lies."

"It's the Maiden," Norman gasped out, "she was kidnapped."

"What?" Michael said in shock.

"You lie!" Crystal scolded him.

"Let him speak, Ulrich!" Michael pleaded. He looked towards Crystal for guidance. She nodded her head and the beast released Norman.

"Sorry, Norman," Michael said as he helped Norman back to his feet, "please tell me what has happened."

Norman stood there for a bit trying to get his breath back. He crouched over, rubbing his neck and coughing. Then he stood up straight and looked right at Ulrich.

"He needs to back up first," Norman said, still gulping down some air. "Go ahead, back up now." Ulrich slowly stepped about ten paces back, then Norman turned his attention back to Michael and Crystal. Norman took a deep breath, "Someone has kidnapped the Maiden of the Seas and my uncle Arthur and I are here to help in the recovery of her."

"That's terrible," Michael said looking at his sister, "how can we help you, Norman?"

"Can you?" Norman asked.

"Can we what?" Crystal intervened.

"Can you help us? It would probably help us a lot if you joined sides with us."

"I don't know, Norman, the Myhr have not really been kind to us."

"It's out of the question," Crystal interrupted. "The Myhr is a brutal race and would kill us if given the chance. I'm sorry, but you do not know the Myhr as we do."

"People change," Norman pleaded, "maybe some form of truce could be made between your two races, giving you access back to Atlantium."

Crystal thought for a moment or two. She looked at her brother and then back out towards the crowds of Crusteans. Who by this time have completely surrounded them and were watching intently. Then she looked back at Norman and shook her head.

"We cannot, but I'll grant you passage back to the gated entrance of our realm."

She walked away from the center and stopped to tell Ulrich something then continued on. Ulrich walked over to Norman. He took a few steps back, intimidated by the large Crustean. This time Ulrich did not touch Norman, instead he beckoned for Norman to follow with a nod of his head. Norman followed Ulrich and headed towards the gate. He heard Michael call out, "good luck," from behind. The trip wasn't long at all. Ulrich left him alone at the gate leading to Atlantium. Norman yelled for help, rattling the bars, and by the third call for help Norman saw some city guards coming towards him.

Escorted by the city guard, Norman stood in the archway to a large open chamber. Inside he could see his uncle with a few Myhr men and an old Myhr woman standing around an ornate table made of coral reef. In the center of the table was a deep basin filled with a blackish blue liquid. Norman's clothes were still damp and cold shivers continued to run through his body. Even with all this happening, Norman's mind was elsewhere. He was thinking about what the Matron had said to him. How was he supposed to rescue the Maiden from the clutches of Mordecai? Who was this Mordecai and what did he want with the Maiden? Norman's mind was spinning out of control, and he didn't notice his uncle wandering over to him.

"Norman, are you okay?" his uncle asked him. Norman jumped a little when his uncle talked to him. He was in a daze and not paying attention.

"What?" Norman said, truly not knowing what his uncle had just said to him. Arthur reached out and put his hand on Norman's shoulder. He felt the cold dampness of Norman's clothes.

"Are you okay?" he asked again. "Why are you so wet?"

"We found him coming out of the Crustean's cave," the guard next to Norman said to Arthur.

"Norman, is this true?" his uncle asked, shocked. Norman lowered his head and couldn't look at his uncle's eyes.

"The Matron had Penelope bring me to her chamber."

"I don't understand, if the Matron called you, then how did you end up with the Crusteans?"

"She showed me things, images in the water."

"What did you see?"

"It was a beautiful tropical island that was destroyed by a wave."

"What do you mean?"

“It was flooded and the buildings that did stick out of the water were destroyed and burned. Then she showed me an image of some man named Mordecai’s stronghold. She said that he has kidnapped the Maiden.”

“So our sources were correct,” Meryck said, slamming his fist into his hand.

“We must make a plan to recover her immediately,” Coulter said.

“Coulter’s right,” Arthur agreed. “If we hope to save the Maiden we must move quickly, before Mordecai knows what hit him.”

“Did the Matron tell you anything else?” Meryck asked Norman.

“She told me that I was to help rescue the Maiden. Then she showed me to a deep hole in the water which led to the Crustean’s cave.”

“She touched you?” a voice bellowed out.

“Yes,” Norman gulped out, not knowing who he was talking to.

“Bring Norman to me, Arthur,” she called back.

Arthur put his arm around Norman’s shoulder and guided him to the large table in the middle of the room. The table was a huge piece of coral reef with the center hollowed out. It was filled with a dark blackish blue liquid, it looked very thick, thicker than water. The old Myhr lady stood between Coutler and Lord Meryck. Her skin was white like first snow fall, as if every ounce of color was drained from her. Her hair was straight and silver, hanging down past her waist. Shiny blue strands of hair were scattered throughout the rest, giving the illusion of flowing water. Her eyes were very strange; they were royal blue without any white in her eyes. When she looked at Norman she seemed to look right into his soul. The only other color on her was on her dress, and it matched her eyes perfectly. When she turned to look at Norman her dress seemed to dance on her frail body.

"Come closer," she beckoned. Norman looked at his uncle for guidance. Arthur nodded his head with approval. The small push on his back also helped. Norman slowly walked around the table towards the old lady. Lord Meryck took a step back to allow for him to pass by. As he got closer to her she reached out for him.

"Let me see your hands, my child."

Norman slowly stretched his arms out towards her. She took both of them into her hands, they were softer than Norman thought they would be. He thought that they would be dry, cracked and old. Her skin was cool to the touch and soft like a satin. Moisture coated her skin. She turned his hands over in hers, examining both sides of his hands. After a little while she raised her head up and gazed into his eyes.

“Who are you?” Norman asked.

“I am Melinda, Norman. I was the old Matron of the Seas. Now I control the Table of Seeing.”

“What’s the Table of Seeing?”

“It is this table that you see before you. It allows me to see things that are happening throughout the oceans.”

“Cool!” was all that Norman could muster up.

“Very cool,” she said with a wink.

“I am sorry to interrupt, you my lady,” Lord Meryck cut in, “of what importance is this boy to us?”

Melinda smiled at Norman then turned her attention back towards the others.

“He has been touched by the Matron. She has transferred some powers to him, to be given to the Maiden.”

“I don’t think it would be safe for Norman to accompany us on this mission,” Arthur intervened.

“I would have to agree with Arthur,” Coulter added. Only Lord Meryck did not oppose Norman’s part in this task. He seemed to look down at Norman with concern in his eyes.

"It does not matter," Melinda quickly responded, "what was given to him can only be given to the Maiden when they touch. It cannot be passed on by any other means."

"Norman," Lord Meryck said, "it seems that there has been a large burden that has been thrust upon your shoulders. I do not wish to increase the weight, but this mission may decide the fate of both our world and yours. Are you willing to help us?"

Norman was fixated on the deep rich voice that came from Lord Meryck's mouth. Everyone else, including Arthur, seemed to turn and focus their attention to Norman. He looked down towards the floor to think, and then looked back up at everyone.

"I'll do it," Norman nervously responded.

"Thank you, Norman," Meryck nodded in his direction, showing his gratitude. "I'll send my personal guard to protect you."

"We'll be leaving first thing tomorrow morning Norman," he added, "so if you wish to get some sleep in your chamber, then you are more than welcome."

"Actually," Norman said, "I would like to walk around the city first. Then maybe get some rest."

"Well, then as soon as we are done with the plans for the mission I'll have my daughter, Regina, give you a tour of the city." With that Meryck nodded towards Melinda. She glanced at Norman then lowered her hand into the pool in the middle of the table. The thick liquid started to glow and then became transparent. Norman stared in amazement at the transformation. Soon after the image of Mordecai's stronghold came into focus, Lord Meryck gave a long and detailed plan on the rescue on the Maiden. Norman listened very closely, trying hard not to forget everything he was supposed to do. It was very hard, he was starting to think about the tour through the city. And his mind was traveling elsewhere.

Chapter Twenty

Jacob and Elizabeth sat on an old dwarf mining contraption called a cave runner. It was a relic from some weird world where science fiction and fantasy clashed with a steam punk twist. They were strapped in one of two black Victorian age sofas that sat behind a single pilot's seat. Günter sat in the pilot seat, a large backed wooden chair, expertly guiding it through the mines with a handful of levers and chains. All the seats were attached to a flat black metal transport shaped like a small boat. The mine trolley empowered with two large green crystals, roared through the royal Alps mining caves that the dwarves of old had dug out. They were suspended by large wheels beneath two metal tracks attached to the side of the cavern wall. Beneath them was nothing but darkness, they could not see the bottom. The rhythmic clunking noise kept putting Jacob to sleep, but Elizabeth couldn't sleep, not after hearing about the death and destruction. Her mind was reeling.

"Günter, how far down have the dwarves dug?"

He sat in front of them trying to concentrate on the track. The tunnel network was made up of thousands of tracks connected by junctions. The junctions allowed for smugglers to make quick changes in any direction to escape authorities. It was a difficult task, seeing as they were traveling ridiculously fast. Travelling at this speed was the only way to smuggle illegal goods, or in this case, people.

"Too deep!" Günter yelled to her. "We would not hit bottom for a long time should we miss a junction. So stop bothering me!" he said with a grunt.

"Well that was pleasant," she told herself. Elizabeth glanced at her husband for someone to keep her company, but he was fast asleep still. She shook her head in disbelief then gave him a light kick to his leg. He jumped a little and opened his eyes.

"Did you just kick me?" he asked.

"No!" she laughed, "a rock must have fallen from the walls."

"Sure," he smiled back at her, "what do you want? I was getting my beauty sleep."

"I've been thinking about the meeting with the elves."

"What about it?"

"I have a bad feeling about this whole situation."

"What do you mean?"

"I think a decision has already been made and the Dark Elves are just trying to follow protocol. Also, I think that the Golden Elves know this, but are trying to gain our assistance by letting us come to their aid."

"Wow, you have been doing a lot of thinking since we left the city. What else are you thinking?"

"What about this thing with the Maiden of the Seas, do you think that Mordecai has acted alone?"

"No, I've been thinking about that since we left Scotland. He must have some support in the shadows."

"Unfortunately, I don't think the Dark Elves are acting alone. I believe that something is wrong in the League of Golden Arrows also."

"Elizabeth, that's a serious accusation," Jacob said astonished. "What makes you think something like that?"

"It is obvious, my love. Only the Golden Arrows knew about the location of Atlantium."

"Oh!"

"Somebody on the inside must have leaked information to either the Dark Elves or Mordecai himself. Unfortunately, that information is not known by all."

"Wow, that's really thick and could get extremely complicated," Jacob said with a shake of his head. Now that she has brought all of this information to the forefront his mind, he was awake now. Just as he realized he was awake, large sparks started flying from the brakes behind their heads. The cave runner was coming to a stop.

“We have arrived,” Günter said as he turned to look at the two of them through goggles that were three sizes too big for his face. All they could do was shake their heads to keep from laughing at his appearance.

“Don’t forget my gold,” he growled at them.

“Günter, my dear,” Elizabeth said in her best soothing voice, “the deal was to deliver us to the gates of Favelyn. As soon as you do I will hand the pouch containing the gold to you.”

“Fine,” he grumbled and pulled a lever allowing the door to swing open.

Günter jumped down onto an old wooden walkway that led into another section of the cave. He did not wait for Jacob or Elizabeth to get down. He just started to walk into the cave.

“Watch your step, humans,” he called back to them, “I would hate to see you fall to your death.”

“I knew he cared,” she said with a laugh.

Chapter Twenty-One

Norman met Lord Meryck's daughter at the bottom of the palace stairs where she was waiting for him. She was dressed in a dark green jumpsuit with a black overcoat. Her hair was bright orange, like a carrot, and she had dimples that seemed to touch when she smiled. She was younger than Norman but yet she was taller than him. When he got to the bottom of the stairs she reached her hand out to greet him. Norman took it and shook it like they were long lost friends. He was starting to get used to meeting new people.

"Hi, my name is Regina," she said. "You must be Norman."

"That's me," he said.

"So what would you like to see?" she asked him.

"All of it if that's possible. If we don't have the time maybe we could just see the coolest spots." Norman seemed to relax around Regina, even though he never met her before. It might have been that she reminded him of his cousin Lilly.

"The entire city is rather big," she told him, "so we'll have to see the coolest spots, as you say."

Norman laughed and followed her as she walked through the city full of buildings made of coral rock. They were surrounded by many large buildings that seemed to be a beehive of activity.

"This is the education district. Just ahead of us we'll come to a big opening and that's the school square. It's just a common area between all of the different buildings that house students. All the Myhr are trained and educated here."

The school square was a very large courtyard with a fountain in the middle. Huge buildings surrounded it on every side with passageways separating them. The buildings were made of beautiful coral rock in all different shades of colors. He liked the way that they never lost the look of a coral reef. They only carved out the inside of the rocks and left the exterior to remain the same as it started.

"This place is awesome," he told her.

"This is nothing," she said to him, "wait until you see where they keep the pods."

"Why wait? Let's go there next."

"Okay, let's see if you can keep up." She took off running out of the square down a passageway. Norman ran after her and soon realized that she was very fast and had trouble keeping up with her. They ran in between people walking down the walkways and they jumped over small obstacles. He was having a very good time, things were so serious lately, and he missed just playing and running around.

They finally came to stop at the only all wooden building Norman had seen in Atlantium. They both stood there for a few seconds breathing very heavily. They looked at each other and then Regina started to laugh. Norman quickly joined in a long session of laughter. When they finished he looked at the enormous wooden building in front of him. It stretched down as far as he could see in one direction, but stopped not too far from him in the other direction. It was two stories high and had a large window every couple of feet, but the windows were closed off with wooden shutters.

"What's this place?" he asked.

"It's the pod house. It covers the edge of most of the eastern side of Lake Knorr. Then it stretches out about thirty feet into the water. Let's go in."

Norman followed her through a large wooden door. When they walked in the scent of fish and salt water was overwhelming. It stopped Norman in his tracks and he had to get used to it. He hid his nose in the inside of his elbow, trying to stop the smell from entering his nose.

"It's only bad by the doorway for some reason. Let's get closer to the water and the smell will fade quite a bit." She led him away from the door; the back of the building didn't exist in some areas. There were huge docks leading out into the middle of the lake. And people were busy all over the place, but he didn't see a giant pod yet. The walls were covered with old fishing gear.

All the way at the end of one of the docks Norman saw a huge boat. He was trying to get a better look when Regina grabbed him by the arm. He looked down and saw that he was standing on the edge of a large square hole in the floor and the water was below.

"Thanks."

"No problem," she said.

"What is that large thing down there?"

"We call them transport pods, they are very similar to human submarines."

"Really? That's so cool!"

"You will use one tomorrow for the rescue mission."

"We're going to ride in that?" he said, astounded. "Wow! Can we go down there and look at it?"

"Sure, just watch your step."

They walked over to the staging area of the transport pod. Norman walked most of the way looking at his feet, not knowing where another hole in the floor would pop up. The floor was littered with different things; crates, barrels, rope, and even buckets full of dead fish. *That's probably where the smell comes from,* he thought to himself.

"What are all these fish for?" Norman asked her.

"Food for the dolphins."

"This is really awesome," he said.

"They are pretty neat," she agreed.

An old man in a tan shirt with brown pants wearing a grey apron walked up to them. He seemed to know who Regina was, but he looked confused about Norman.

"How can I help you, Regina?" he asked. He sounded like a grumpy old man to Norman.

"I'm showing Norman around the city, Eric."

"Well, this place isn't a playground, be careful."

"We will," she responded.

"Come on, Norman," she said, "I have somewhere else very cool to bring you. If you thought this place smelled bad, wait until we get to this next place."

"Well, in that case, I can't wait."

They left the building and then took off on another race through the city. This time they seemed to be running downhill. They passed through a section that looked like people's houses. These buildings were small in comparison to the other places of business and learning. He saw different kinds of sea plants in the windows. As they came around a corner they came to a large complex of more wooden and coral buildings. There were about thirty buildings surrounding a huge lake. Norman's nose suddenly caught the scent of fish.

"You were right, this place smells like a seafood counter at the supermarket!" Norman told her.

"What's a supermarket?" she asked.

"It's a place where we buy food, and trust me the seafood counter smells bad. What is this place?"

"These are the fish farms. It's where we raise fish to supply the homes with food. We also grow vegetables in these buildings. They use the water that the fish are in to help the food grow. In Lake Aryell we grow kelp which is used to make our clothes."

"Is that Lake Aryell?" Norman asked pointing to the huge lake that the buildings sat around.

"Yes, it is," she said, "Come on, Norman, it's getting late and I promised my father I wouldn't keep you out too long. He said that you have a huge day tomorrow and spent most of last night awake."

Norman agreed unwillingly and followed her back to the palace. She showed him to his chambers and wished him luck on the next day's mission. Just like that, she was gone, and he was alone in a large, cold bedroom.

Chapter Twenty Two

Norman stood in his room looking out the window over the city of Atlantium. He was thinking about all that had happened so far this summer. He knew that no one would believe the tales about this place and their adventures so far. The family would probably call him crazy, especially his cousin Lilly. She already calls his uncle crazy and now Norman was living out those crazy tales. "*This was not your normal summer*," he thought to himself.

"The whole place is one efficient machine," Norman said out loud. Everything had a purpose and place. The light tubes in the cavern started to dim and house lights flickered on one by one. Norman walked over and turned the light on next to his bed. He crawled onto his bed and sat with his back against the headboard. There was a pitcher of water sitting on the bedside table with a glass next to it. There was also an envelope with his name on it. He picked up the letter and turned it over, wondering who had sent it since there wasn't any other name on it. The paper inside had a bunch of weird symbols on it. Then Norman remembered the Golden Arrow decoder. These were the same symbols that wrapped around it.

Norman pulled the decoder and a pencil out of his green army bag. He walked over to a desk in the corner of the room and looked for a number around the edge of the paper. He found a number II in the bottom left corner. After turning the gold arrow to point at the number II on the decoder, he decoded the message.

"Norman," the letter read, "I wanted to tell you that we'll be leaving in the middle of the night. So have your bag packed and ready to go. Secrecy is extremely important because the royal family thinks there are spies in the city. I will come for you when it is time to go. Get some rest, you will need it. Sincerely, Uncle Arthur."

He walked back over after reading the letter and grabbed the pitcher. He poured a glass of water. Images of his mother and father filled his head while drifting to sleep.

"Norman"

Norman heard his name being called but couldn't see who was calling out to him. There was a grey mist swirling around and a terrible chill in the air. The smell of wood burning filled his nostrils. He paused not wanting to walk further into the mist.

"Hello, is anybody out there?" he called out.

"Norman," the voice called out again.

This time Norman knew the voice, his mother. She was the one calling out to him. He raced into the mist looking in every direction but couldn't find her.

"Mom," he shouted out.

"Norman, help us," she pleaded.

"MOM!" he shouted again.

How was she here in Atlantium? She was supposed to be in Europe with his father. His heart was racing and pounding through his chest. He continued to run blind through the mist.

“Mom, where are you?” he continued to yell out.

Then without a warning he ran off some sort of ledge but he still couldn’t see. He just fell through the mist. Then he woke in the bed kicking and thrashing. He was breathing hard and covered in sweat. It took a few seconds to realize that he was still in the room in Atlantium.

“Mom,” he called out into the darkness.

“*Someone must have turned the light off*,” he thought. He couldn’t see a thing, the room was so dark. Norman slowly fell back to sleep, thinking of his mother again. Norman slept soundly through the rest of the night without another bad dream.

Chapter Twenty Three

Norval stood in the rain just outside Faneuil Hall marketplace in Boston, Massachusetts. He wore a dark grey wool long coat. His hat was pulled down low and water dripped off the rim. A dark figure approached him from the shadows. The lone light-post he stood near kept the stranger's face in the shadow.

"Who goes there?" Norval called out.

"Calm yourself, Councilman Needles," Fayne said to him. "Did you bring the artifact that I've requested?"

"Of course I did," he said, reaching into his pocket. He pulled out a small item wrapped in a brown handkerchief. He held it out to Fayne with hesitation, "What will happen to Jacob and Elizabeth?"

The dark elf walked to him and took the small item from his hands. Fayne undid the cloth and held a golden ring up into the light. A ruby in the shape of a skull was set into the top of it. A dark magic swirled in the center of the gem and a wicked smile spread across the elf's face. He dropped the ring into his breast pocket with a soft pat to ensure its safety.

"I have told you before, don't you worry about them two, I will handle them."

"I don't want any more death."

"They have the scrolls," Fayne said, getting into Norval's face, "I will kill a thousand to get those scrolls and a thousand more if need be."

"Get your scrolls! Do not harm the Skylairs," Norval said and walked away into the darkness. Shortly after, another dark elf guard came out of the shadows and stood beside Fayne. He bowed and looked after the councilman.

"What are your orders?" he asked Fayne.

"Keep a close eye on our dear friend Norval."

"Yes, sir."

"I feel that his usefulness may be wearing thin."

"We will need someone new in the League."

"That has already been arranged; do not worry yourself with such matters."

"As you wish, should I bring an enchantress with me?"

"No, bring a blood elf if you need to. All our enchantresses are working to awaken a shadow dragon for the Skylairs."

The guard was noticeably shaken and he took a step back. The air grew colder with just the talk of shadow dragons. Shadow dragons are the embodiment of hatred and fear. They move amongst the shadows and through one's nightmares. The flames of destruction produced by a shadow dragon can drain the energy of life from you.

"The shadow dragons have not been awakened for a thousand years," the guard responded to Fayne.

"I know this," Fayne reiterated. "We must have the scrolls if we are to ever wipe out this infection called humans."

"With all due respect, sir, shadow dragons cannot be controlled."

"Enough, follow the councilman. I will get you a message when it is time. Until then just watch him and make sure he doesn't give away our plans to the other council members."

"I understand," the dark elf bowed and turned to leave.

***

"Norman," Arthur called while shaking his shoulders, "Norman, wake up. We have to leave now."

Norman's eyes sprung open and he jolted up in bed. He almost banged his head on the headboard of the bed. His feet hit the floor before he realized that he was awake.

"What's wrong, what's going on?" Norman asked his uncle.

“Didn’t you get my message?” he asked, “we are leaving for Mordecai’s stronghold.”

“Oh yeah,” Norman said, shaking the sleep from his head, “I just forgot.”

Norman grabbed his bag from the floor next to the bed and followed his uncle out of the room. They moved quickly down the corridor and through a passageway that was concealed behind a large tapestry. The passageway was a narrow stairwell that almost led straight down. It was very dark and Norman was trying very hard not to slip. The walls and the floor had a thin layer of moisture on it; just like everything else in Atlantium. It was dimly lit by some torches every thirty or forty feet.

“Where are we going?” Norman asked his uncle.

“This is a secret set of stairs leading to the royal family’s personal docks.”

“What’s there?”

“The transport pods.”

“Awesome,” Norman said with excitement growing. Arthur stopped and turned towards the child.

“Norman, I know the idea of riding in a submarine is exciting, but these are very dangerous times. Make no mistake; Mordecai will not welcome us with open arms when we arrive at the stronghold.”

“I am sorry, Uncle Arthur.”

“No, Norman, don’t be sorry about that. It is important to be excited about things in life. I just didn’t want you to forget about the dangers ahead of us.”

Arthur turned back around and continued down the stairs. It didn’t take them much longer until they reached the bottom of the stairs. They went through a large door which led to the royal docks. There were two huge transport pods, one in front of the other. The docks were busy with people getting the pods ready. There were two large metal gangplanks that were walkways from the docks to the entry hatches of the pods. The walkways rose up and down with the bobbing of the pods. Norman watched as different Myhr gathered their gear. After gathering it all they would climb into the pods and disappear from Norman’s view. Norman started to feel some butterflies in his stomach. This was all becoming very real now.

“What do we need to do?” Norman asked his uncle.

“I just need to find Coulter and see which transport we’ll be riding in.”

His uncle was looking around the docks for Captain Coulter. He was standing by some crates being loaded. Arthur walked over to him with Norman just a foot behind.

“Good morning, Coulter,” Arthur said as he shook his hand, “Is everything running smoothly?”

“Yes,” Coulter responded, “everything seems to be moving smoothly.”

“Where will Norman and I be riding?”

“You’ll be in the lead transport,” he said pointing to the front pod.

“Excuse me, sir, is there anything I need to get or do?” Norman asked Coulter.

“Norman, there is a bag in your transport with the only gear you should need in it. You’ll meet up with Milton in there and he’ll give it to you.”

“I never fired a gun before,” Norman said to his uncle.

“And you won’t fire one now,” he responded.

“Oh no, Norman, we don’t use weapons like that. Ours will only stun people and you’ll not even have one of them. You are under the protection of the royal family’s private guard. Milton is their captain and will be by your side the entire time. The rest of us will create the diversion while you slip into their pipe system. Your team will actually be quite small compared to the surface assault group.”

“Let’s get into the pod, Norman,” his uncle said, guiding him away.

"Oh, Arthur, a message came from Lady Meara. She said that she will meet you on the surface," Coulter called out. Arthur stopped and turned around when he heard him.

"Good," Arthur replied and continued into the pod.

"So we're going to meet with Lady Meara again?" Norman inquired.

"She'll be there when the sub surfaces, but I'm not sure if you will still be with us. Your team may leave the sub prior to the arrival. Remember what Lord Meryck said about your entry into the pipe system; it must remain stealth. No one can know of your rescue."

"Wow, I sure wish I could see her again."

"I know," Arthur said with a smile, "she sure is beautiful."

They climbed long metal gangplanks and entered into the pod. The first room was exceptionally empty compared to the amount of people that got on board before him. Norman followed his uncle through a hatchway in the back of the room. It opened into a large room with a bunch of chairs in it. They were the same kind of chairs that Norman remembered from riding in an airplane.

"Let's sit over there, Norman," Arthur said pointing to two empty chairs in the corner next to a small circular window. Norman followed his uncle's finger and started to make his way over to the chairs.

"I'll meet you there," he called out to him.

"Okay," Norman responded.

Norman walked over and took the seat closest to the window so that he could look out of it while they traveled through the water. Norman glanced around at the Myhr in the room. He could feel an unseen energy buzzing through the air. He didn't think that they were excited about what they were doing, more like just excited to be finally getting it over with. Norman was so busy looking around at all the different people that he didn't notice the Myrh standing right in front of him.

"Norman," he said.

"Hello, I didn't even see you come up."

"Sorry about that, Norman, my name is Milton. I'm the captain of the Maiden's private guards and we'll make sure you reach her safely. Here, this belongs to you," he said as he handed Norman an old brown messenger bag. Norman took it and glanced inside the bag.

"Thanks," he told Milton.

"Go ahead and take it out."

"Okay."

Norman removed a green rod with leather straps wrapped around one end making a handgrip. The other half of the rod was made of some type of green stone. It was extremely smooth and flawless. The tip at the end was in the shape of a small fist. It was just over eight inches long. Norman turned it over in his hand a couple of times.

"What is it?" Norman asked wide-eyed.

"That's a blast rod, Norman. Your uncle didn't want you to go into the battle empty-handed. So keep it in the bag or in one of your cargo pockets."

"What does it blast?"

"When you thrust it at your enemy it will increase the impact by about tenfold. They will probably be thrown through the air."

"That must be cool to see," Norman gasped.

"Maybe, but it probably doesn't feel that cool for them. Make sure you keep it hidden and safe."

"This is so awesome," Norman said, "I've never seen stuff like this before."

"Really cool stuff, huh?" Arthur said as he walked up next to Norman and sat down in his seat.

"Hey, thanks for the blast rod, Uncle Arthur"

"No problem," Arthur said, "that's one of the reasons we stopped in Newport. The rod was a gift from my mentor, Silverfox,"

Arthur told Norman, “he trained me when I was a young Golden Arrow.”

“Silverfox?”

“Silverfox was his nickname,” Arthur said.

“How did he get it?”

“When he was a young man he went on a mission into Siberia. When he came back his hair had turned to a silver color. He never told anybody what happened, but he never went back to the Alps. He was a brilliant and brave man, I learned quite a bit from him.”

“We are about to move away from the docks,” the intercom system squawked. “All hands prepare to get underway.”

“Here we go, Norman,” Arthur said.

The boat seemed to lunge to the side and then balanced out moving forward. It was a weird sensation to feel at first. After a while Norman got used to the motion and didn’t even feel it anymore.

Chapter Twenty Four

It felt like they were traveling forever, even though it was only an hour and a half. Norman was getting very bored and he wanted to see the ship. He put all of his new gear into his army bag, then got up to take another look out of the porthole window next to his chair. The water was a lighter blue, but it was still rather hard to see anything out there.

"Where are you going?" his uncle asked him.

"I was just going to walk around the ship and see what there is to see," he told him.

"All right, just make sure you stay out of the crew's way. They have to run the ship and that can be very difficult."

"I will."

Arthur laid his head back against the seat and closed his eyes for a little while. Norman took that as his cue to leave and start some exploring. The pod had become a little more crowded since he first got onboard. Norman didn't know where anything was, but that would be half the adventure. He slipped the rod into his right cargo pocket and walked back through the door that led into the first room. Across the room sat another door with a ladder leading down. He walked over to it and peered inside. He saw that the ladder went up and down. The ladder was painted blue and bolted to the wall, it stuck out about four inches from it. Norman grabbed on with his left hand and swung out to the ladder. He sat there for a second or two trying to decide which way to go, up or down. He looked up first then looked below, shrugging his shoulders he headed down the ladder. Besides, in all the stories most dungeons are down. He figured something cool must be down there. It didn't take long before he got to the next floor. The sign next to the door leading out read '2nd Deck,' the sign looked like it could glow in the dark if need be. He decided to keep climbing down a little further, since he was having fun just climbing at the moment.

The descent to the bottom introduced Norman to the 3rd, 4th, 5th, and finally the 6th Deck. The bottom of the ladderwell was a hard steel deck. He walked through the door into the adjoining compartment. It was very hot and humid in this room and he could see moisture forming on the walls. The noise was almost deafening, there were tremendous machines throughout the compartment with spinning wheels and belts.

"This must be some kind of engine room or something like that," Norman spoke softly to himself. He was a little confused because he didn't see anybody down here. The room was completely empty. Well, as far as he could see, at least. Norman continued to walk further into the room, wondering where everyone was.

“Aaahhh,” Norman yelled as a blast of steam came out of a pipe near him. Luckily it wasn’t shooting directly at him or he probably would‘ve been burned. He kept on walking forward with his heart moving a little faster now. He was starting to get nervous. The hairs were standing up on the back of his neck and sweat was starting to drip off his brow.

“Is anybody in here?” Norman called. He waited patiently to hear if someone would respond, but there was no response. He walked up to a large machine and turned to look down the gap between it and the machine next to it. Norman’s heart dropped to the floor; there was a Myhr lying on the floor. He was half under the machine and half in the walkway. He didn’t know what to do. He looked back towards the door and didn’t see anyone. When he looked back he jumped, startled, the body was being slowly dragged under the machine. Norman was afraid; he tried to move, but his feet were cemented to the ground. All he could think about at the moment was to just scream for help. He was worried that whatever was pulling on the body might hear him.

“Help me!” Norman yelled as somebody grabbed his right shoulder. He jumped straight up and spun around in the air, to see a Myhr standing behind him. He was wearing a navy blue jumpsuit and was covered from head to toe in what seemed to be grease. Even with all the grease covering him, the Myhr’s emerald green eyes shined through.

“What are you doing down here?” he asked Norman.

"I was just exploring around the ship."

"Well it isn't safe down here and you need to get back up to the main deck. The rest of your team may be looking…"

"Sir," Norman interrupted, "there is somebody injured down here."

"What do you mean?"

Norman turned around to show him what he was talking about but he didn't see the body there anymore. Whoever it was, they had been carried off.

"There was a body on the floor just over there," Norman said pointing to the spot where the body was just a moment ago.

"I don't see anything," the Myhr stated.

"Trust me sir, it was there and it was being dragged off under the machinery," he tried to convince the Myhr.

"Let me go and see," he said. He walked down the walkway between the machines, looking side-to-side to see if there was a body. He came to the spot where Norman had pointed and stopped in his tracks. His assistant, Cullard, was lying flat on his back. His face was completely drained of any color and contorted in fear. He looked up from the body and almost fainted. In front of him was a hideous being. Its skin was a shiny black and the eyes were blood red with strands of skin imprisoning them. The monster opened its mouth revealing way too many razor sharp fangs. The Myhr man turned and started to run towards Norman.

"A blood elf!" he yelled. "Runnn!"

No sooner did the words 'run' get out of his mouth, the blood elf slammed him against the machine. Norman stood looking at the monster. He was fumbling with the pocket on his leg trying to get the blast rod free. It slowly looked up at Norman with an evil grin. Norman started running towards the ladder, pulling the rod out as he ran. Norman didn't stop to look back. He launched his body through the doorway and started up from the fifth rung. He was racing up the ladder as fast as he could, after he passed the sign that said '5th Deck' he looked back to see where the monster was. Unfortunately it was closing the gap.

"Somebody help me!" Norman shouted at the top of his lungs. "HELP!" he yelled again and again. Myhr heads started to poke out of the doorways. Norman could see the look of shock on all of their faces. Immediately after the first person saw the blood elf, red lights started flashing and an alarm blared. Norman reached for the next rung and felt cold fingers grab his right ankle and they started pulling him downward. A vicious growl came from the beast, it was inching closer to Norman with its razor sharp teeth bared and ready to rip him to shreds.

"Norman!" Arthur yelled from the main deck. Norman looked up and saw his uncle starting to climb down the ladder. Norman didn't know what to do, he was losing his grip and he was terrified! He looked at his hands and remembered the blasting rod. He let go with his right hand, which held the blasting rod. Then turned to look at the blood elf; his left hand was losing its grip quickly. Norman flipped the blast rod over in his hand so the ball at the end was facing the blood elf. The monsters head leaned to the side as if trying to figure out what Norman had. By the time the beast realized what the boy had, it was too late. Norman slammed it down into the elf's forehead with a loud thunderous clap. The blood elf shot down the ladder spinning in a perfect spiral and landing in a crumpled pile on the bottom deck. Norman started racing up the ladder to his uncle. Arthur leaned to the side while Norman passed by him.

"Go straight to the room that we were sitting in," he told Norman. Norman didn't question him and went straight up the ladder. When he got to the top he looked down towards the bottom. He was shocked to see that the blood elf was gone. His uncle and many others were flooding into the machinery room at the bottom. Norman ran into the passenger room and went to his seat. He sat there looking out the window trying to calm his nerves. It didn't help any, because he saw the evil thing swimming away from the boat. He was glued to the spot and couldn't take his eyes off it. Then the elf stopped and turned back looking straight at Norman. It started swimming back to the transport pod. Now full of fear, Norman still couldn't turn from the window. The elf swam with speed that Norman had never seen before and within seconds it was face to face with Norman, the only thing separating them was the piece of glass. The blood elf slammed its fist on the outside wall, making the sound of a loud hollow thud. Its fiery red eyes were filled with hatred and evil. A large indentation was right in the center of its forehead. It glared at Norman for what seemed like forever.

People started to file back into the room behind Norman. Seeing this, the elf gave one last look at Norman and swam off. Norman felt a knot in his stomach; somehow he knew that they would be crossing paths again. The lights and the alarm finally stopped. Norman turned away from the window and sat in his seat. After about fifteen minutes Uncle Arthur walked back into the room and went straight to the chair next to Norman. Sitting down, he let out a big sigh of relief.

"The blood elf is gone! Unfortunately we couldn't catch him," his uncle informed him.

"How are the two Myhr men?" he asked his uncle.

"The engineer is fine; his assistant is being tended to."

"Will he be okay?"

"That's hard to tell, the elf cast fear into him. And that is usually very fatal. The Myhr are tending to him for now and we are going to make an emergency surfacing to find the elves. Only they can truly counter the spell cast on him."

"Uncle Arthur, I was really afraid down there."

"So was I, Norman, so was I!" Arthur said putting a hand on Norman's knee. "I'm sure that you really did a number on that thing's face with your blast rod."

"That was pretty cool," Norman agreed.

"Norman, I'm very proud of you right now, you're able to think in a crisis. You're going to grow up to make all of us proud," Arthur ruffled his hand through Norman's hair.

"Including your parents," he added.

Norman felt a lump form in his throat with the mention of his parents. He missed them terribly and he worried about their trip. It brought his dream back to his thoughts. He wondered about asking his uncle's opinion, but figured there was enough going on right now and he didn't want to add to it.

"Do you think that my parents are okay?" Norman asked instead.

"I'm sure they are fine," he told him, "I used to get your father and me in some really sticky situations. He always made sure we came out on top."

Norman felt a little better knowing this but he couldn't get that feeling out of his stomach. Coulter came walking up to Norman and Arthur. He took the seat across from Arthur.

"Arthur we need to talk about the blood elf."

"What are you thinking?" Arthur asked him.

"Why was he on the transport pod? Are there more back at Atlantium? And are they involved with this kidnapping, anyway?"

Norman just sat and watched as the two adults talked about today's events. He was replaying it over in his head as well.

"We have ordered the other pod back to Atlantium. They'll inform Lord Meryck of the blood elf and possible threat," Coulter told Arthur.

"I hope that helps," Arthur said.

"Is something on your mind?" Coulter asked.

"I was thinking that if Mordecai has elicited the assistance of the blood elves, then we may have a ton of trouble waiting for us and we may be heading into a storm. Our problems may run deeper than just this kidnapping. Something bigger is probably happening."

"Do you believe Lord Meryck's concerns about spies in Atlantium?"

"It's possible."

"How can that be, we are secluded from the world. Only the Golden Arrows know of us and they have been our allies for nearly a century."

“Unfortunately, some people within the league may not hold the same values of the league. That’s why I left it ten years ago.”

Chapter Twenty Five

The Maiden was strapped to a wooden chair in the middle of a dark room. The only light in the room shined directly down on her. She was tired and sore, her head hung down until her chin rested on her chest. James stood next to her with his hand on her shoulder. He just waited for Mordecai to show up with the new guest.

"When my boss gets here, you are in trouble, Your Highness," he said with sarcasm dripping from the last two words.

"I don't care," the Maiden told him, "I will not do anything else for that mad man. He's wasting his time."

"We will see."

Just then the door opened, and Mordecai and another gentleman entered the room. The Maiden raised her head and looked at the guest. She didn't know who he was but he didn't look like he was a friend of hers. His skin was very smooth with a tint of grey to it. His eyes were black as night and he had long shiny black hair. It was the ears that intrigued her, they had a small point at the top, just enough to be noticed.

Mordecai stopped in front of the Maiden and raised her chin to look into her eyes. He could see hatred in her eyes and malice towards him. He just smiled at her casually, not even caring.

"I would like to introduce you to a friend of ours," he told her.

"Any friend of yours is an enemy of mine!" she spat at him.

"You may be right, child," he said with a shrug, "but it doesn't matter, soon I will have what I want and you will have worn out your usefulness."

"What are you talking about?"

"This is Fayne, he is a dark elf. He has brought me an artifact that will allow me to take the power to control the ocean from you."

Mordecai turned partway around and reached out his hand towards the dark elf. Fayne pulled out a gold ring with a large red gem on the top of it. Along the band and around the gem itself there were ancient runes and symbols carved into it.

"How does it work?" Mordecai asked Fayne. The dark elf rolled his eyes at the question but Mordecai was unable to see the reaction.

"Turn the gem counter clockwise. Then you'll see the small needle come out of the middle of the gem. You have to insert directly into the birthmark."

“Then what will happen then?”

“It will draw blood into the runes and they will use the power from her to enchant the gem.”

“I’ll be able to control the oceans then?” Mordecai asked Fayne.

“Yes and no,” Fayne continued. “Unlike her, you will only be able to control the water that you see.”

“Why?”

“She’s born with the ability,” he told him, “you are just borrowing it.”

Mordecai looked at the Maiden with a form of greed in his eyes. His want for power was unmatched. He would do anything to be the most powerful person in the room. The Maiden was scared.

“You have something for me,” Fayne asked with extreme interest.

“Unfortunately, I don’t,” Mordecai said with great disappointment, “but we know the whereabouts.”

“We had a deal! You were supposed to acquire the scroll from the Skylairs,” Fayne told him with venom in his voice.

“We searched their house, their business and even used a lot of resources to get into some safety deposit boxes at their bank. The scroll was nowhere to be found.”

“Did you not just tell me you knew where it is?”

“Yes, there is a room in the back of their store. The door is warded with magical enchantments. We couldn’t get through it but I am sure that you will be able to break the enchantments.”

“You can count on it,” Fayne told him. *The scrolls are now within our reach*, the Dark Elf thought to himself.

Chapter Twenty Six

The transport pod burst through the surface of the ocean like a mountain of steel. A cascade of waterfalls ran off every angle on the pods. Everyone was inside either strapped down or holding onto something, waiting for that moment. Within a few seconds the crew was opening the hatch and climbing to the outside walkways.

Coulter was one of the first to make his way outside the vessel; he squinted his eyes when the sunlight first hit him. Milton and Arthur joined him on the walkway shortly afterwards.

"Can you see the cloud of mist yet?" Arthur asked him.

"Nothing yet," Coulter told him.

"We are early because of the emergency ascent to the surface," Milton added, "the elves are never late."

"I know," Arthur agreed.

They were all too busy scanning the horizon that they didn't even notice Norman come out to meet them. The warm sun brought a smile to Norman as it touched his face. It had been a few days since they left the surface and the salty air was very welcoming.

"What is everyone looking at?" Norman asked. The three of them jumped a little at the sound of his voice. Arthur put one hand on Norman's shoulder and the other on his chest.

"You can't come sneaking up on me like that, Norman. I am not as young as I used to be," his uncle told him.

"I am sorry," Norman said, "but what are you looking at?"

"What are we looking at?" his uncle repeated to himself. "We are searching for a cloud of mist."

"Why?"

"Because that will let us know that the *Mist Traveler* is near. The water elves travel cloaked in a cloud to hide them from humans."

"Really?" Norman gasped.

"Unfortunately you were sleeping when the elves arrived and met us on the *Sandra Gale* that morning or you would have seen the magic unfold," his uncle reminded him.

"I remember," agreed Norman, "I woke up and they were already on your ship."

Norman gazed past his uncle and scanned the horizon hoping to catch a glimpse of the mist that they just told him about. However, Coulter was the first to notice the large and nearly opaque cloud floating towards them from a distance. Norman suddenly came to the realization that he would be seeing Lady Meara once again. The thought of this made his stomach start to feel a little weird and his face felt warm on the cheeks. He didn't understand the feelings he was having but they made him nervous and excited at the same time.

"Norman," Milton called out, jarring Norman from his thoughts.

"Yeah," Norman responded.

"Go and gather your gear, we'll be departing from a location on the bottom of the transport pod. We must hurry before the elves get here."

"What?" Norman said shocked.

"We must leave without their knowledge, Norman," Milton informed him, "the entire race of elves is connected magically to their brethren in some form and we cannot take the chance of compromising our mission. If the water elves learn of our plans then there is a possibility that the dark elves may learn of the plan."

"Darn," Norman said. His shoulders dropped down a little and he lightly kicked the deck while he looked down. His uncle could only smile while he watched Norman's reaction. He took Norman by the shoulders and looked into his eyes.

"If you want me to, I'll tell Lady Meara that you were hoping to see her again. Unfortunately, you have urgent matters that you must attend to. Does that sound important enough to miss her arrival?" his uncle asked him.

"Okay," Norman gave in.

"Norman, I'll meet you in the large entry room in a little bit, then take you to the dive pool, where we will exit the boat," Milton told him as he walked back into the boat.

"All right, I'll be right there," Norman called back to him. Norman looked up at his uncle then back out at the mist one more time. He let out a deep breath and walked back into the transport pod. He made his way past Myrh people. All of them were getting ready for the mission ahead of them. He stood in the large room gazing out a porthole at the sunlight. Shortly after that Milton walked up next to Norman.

"All right, let's get out of here."

"Okay," Norman told him.

Milton led the way back to the ladderwell that Norman went down when he met the blood elf, except they got off one deck sooner. They walked down a long passageway which led them to another ladderwell. This ladder led them even further down into the belly of the transport pod. Norman looked into each room they passed with amazement. They finally ended at a large room with a pool of water in the middle of the floor. The dark blue water was licking the edges of the pool with the bobbing of the pod. Milton turned to Norman and gave him a silly smirk; there were five other Myrh already in the room.

"We will be riding dolphin gliders to Mordecai's stronghold. Get ready for some fun!" Milton told him.

"What's a dolphin glider?" Norman asked.

"You'll see," Milton said, smiling. "Here, put this on and then get into the pool."

Milton handed him a small leather strap that wrapped around Norman's forearm. It was plain brown worn leather with a small buckle on the underside, like a watch. On the top there was a purple crystal embedded into it.

"What is it?" Norman asked.

"It will produce a barrier of air between you and the water."

"Do you mean like an air bubble?"

"Yes, like an air bubble that is the exact shape of your body and you will be able to breathe underwater because of it."

"This is so awesome!" Normal stated.

"Grab the helmet on the table, it will allow you to communicate with us in the water." Milton disappeared beneath the surface of the water. Norman finished latching on the strap around his arm, then stuck his hand into the water and pulled it out. The skin was completely dry, not a drop of water anywhere.

"Awesome," Norman awed.

He picked up the helmet and looked it over. It didn't resemble any normal helmet that Norman had seen before. It was a leather skullcap with two glass bubbles covering his ears and two covering his eyes. He slid the contraption on and felt ridiculous. The reflection could be seen in the water and it did look ridiculous. Norman just shrugged his shoulders and plunged into the pool. Arthur wouldn't be coming with him on this mission, but that just dawned on him. It was making him a little nervous, but he knew he had to do it. Soon he was surrounded by water and yet he was completely dry. There were bright lights underneath the transport pod that illuminated the entire area. Milton was next to a dolphin with some odd gear on it. It resembled the triangle hand grips on a hang glider and it looped up around the head of the dolphin by its dorsal fin. There was another bar behind the dorsal fin that looped around the beginning of the tail and formed an upside down "T" underneath the dolphin. Norman was truly excited now and couldn't wait to try it out.

"Can you hear me?" Milton asked. His voice came to Norman as if there wasn't an ocean separating them. It felt as if they were just sitting on a couch talking.

"I can hear, actually," Norman told him, "and see really good, too!"

"Are you ready to get going?"

"Yes, let's go," Norman responded.

Norman swam over to the side of the dolphin that Milton was by. Milton took Norman's hands and showed him where to grab the bar at the base of the triangle. Then he helped him get his feet up on the T-bar, at the tail of the dolphin. Norman was now parallel to the body of the dolphin. Norman watched as the rest of the Myrh got situated on their dolphins.

"Here we go," Milton told everyone. "Hold on Norman, they go pretty fast."

"Okay," was all that Norman could get out before the dolphins took off like lightning through the sea. The water rushed past Norman's head and it sounded a little strange. As soon as they travelled past the reach of the lights from the transport pod, the water became dark again. Norman had to trust that the dolphins knew where they were going.

Chapter Twenty Seven

Norman glided through the water under his dolphin. He could see the other Myhr riding along with him. The ocean seemed very peaceful and serene; it made Norman wonder about what was ahead of them. He couldn't tell for sure, but it looked like there were other Myhr coming with them just outside of his field of vision. They must have been on dolphin gliders as well, he thought to himself.

"Milton, are there other Myhr with us here?" he asked.

"No, Norman, it is just the six of us right here," Milton's voiced burst from the internal microphones in the helmet.

"Really…"

"What's wrong, Norman?"

"It's nothing; I just thought I saw someone or something swimming alongside of us."

"They are sharks, Norman."

"Sharks! Are they following us?"

"Yes, they are following us, but they won't come anywhere near us, Norman. You have nothing to fear as long as you're on your dolphin glider."

"Why would they be following us?"

"They must be hungry."

Norman couldn't help but laugh when Milton told him that they were hungry. It didn't take long for Norman to realize that he was the only one laughing. Suddenly his silent air bubble didn't feel so safe.

"What do you mean they're hungry?"

"Sharks hunt down Myhr and eat them. We are a natural enemy of the sharks."

"That's disgusting!"

"I would have to agree with you, the sharks have learned that our transports carry a source of food for them. So they follow it and hunt the waters near it."

"Will they attack us?"

"No, the sharks are afraid of the dolphins. As long as we are on the gliders we will be safe."

Norman tried not to think of the sharks that were swimming around them. Unfortunately, he imagined them licking their teeth, if sharks were able to do that. When he first got into the water and climbed onto the dolphin glider he was worried about the outcome at the stronghold. Now he was a little bit more concerned about being eaten by a hungry shark. As much as he tried, he couldn't get his mind off the possibility. Norman kept his eyes on the other people that were in his group. That's when he noticed the movement out of the corner of his eye. The sharks seemed to be moving in closer, and then they would swim out again, as if they were testing the perimeter.

"I think the sharks are really starving, because they seem to be getting closer."

"Norman, try not to worry," Milton responded.

"I can't help it," he told him, "these sharks are definitely not afraid of our dolphins and all I have protecting me is an air bubble! "

"I think your fears are making you think that the sharks are getting closer and your air bubble is very safe because it is magic."

"Milton, watch out…" no sooner had Norman got the words out, a large bull shark came at Milton with its mouth wide open. Milton responded quickly, slamming his fist into the gills of the shark causing it to swim off towards the ocean floor. Norman's internal helmet speakers blew up with chatter from all of the Myhr in his group.

"Everyone get a hold of yourselves!" Milton cut in. "Keep your eyes open for more shark attacks."

“Are you okay?” Norman asked.

“Yes, thanks to you, Norman, I am safe for now. Something is making the sharks act like this; they would never venture into a school of dolphins knowingly.”

Norman reached into his pocket and pulled out his blast rod. He held it close to the hand that kept him on the dolphin glider. All of his senses were at full alert; every movement caused him to look around in every direction. He started to think that he could hear the different sounds of the ocean and he was trying to hear the sharks swimming closer. It was obvious that the other members of his group felt the same way. They were constantly turning their heads in all directions.

Suddenly, as expected, the same large bull shark exploded out of the darkness and slammed into a Myhr and dolphin to the right of Norman. The Myhr lost his footing and his feet swung down below him. Norman looked around with a feeling of helplessness. “*Where is the shark?*” he thought. As if on cue, the shark came around for another run and was heading straight for the Myhr’s legs. Just before it could get him, Milton’s dolphin glider slammed its long nose into the gills of the shark. The shark rolled over a couple of times and swam away right past Norman.

Norman spun around, trying to see where it went just as his dolphin jerked up to move out of the way of the shark. He lost his grip on the blast rod and it started to drift downward. He looked down and tried to reach out to grab it, which caused him to lose his footing and grip on the dolphin glider. Norman felt his heart jump into his throat as he fell away from the dolphin, but he did find some comfort as he wrapped his fingers around the blast rod.

He looked around to get his bearing and he could see that the other dolphins and their riders had scattered to avoid the shark attacks. Norman could hear his heart pounding in his ears as he frantically searched for the bull shark and his dolphin glider. Unfortunately, he saw the shark first; it was coming straight for him with what seemed to be a smirk on its face. Norman pulled his feet up to his chest just as the shark closed its mouth on the water below him. He turned just in time to see Milton racing back to him with Norman's glider following close behind. Norman reached out and hooked his arm into the handle at the bottom of the dolphin, and just as he did the shark clamped down on his dolphin's fin on the right side. Norman's dolphin spun frantically trying to escape the sharks grip, whipping Norman left and right. Reaching his other arm straight out, Norman swung the blast rod into one of the bull shark's beady little black eyes.

Norman thought he heard a faint scream from the shark somewhere behind the loud clapping sound of the blast rod. The shark let go of the dolphin and swam off, most likely not to return. Norman crawled onto his glider as the whole group took off like lightening.

"Are you okay, Norman?"

"I-I think so," Norman stuttered.

“Looks like I needed you for the protection.”

“Thanks.”

“No, thank you, Norman, now let’s go get the Maiden before it’s too late.”

Chapter Twenty Eight

Jacob and Elizabeth followed behind Günter as he led the way out of the mines and through a forest. They came to a large clearing on the mountainside and could see for miles. Far below them was a beautiful river and on the opposite bank was a timeless looking town. A large lush forest lay between them and the river.

"Is that the City of Chur?" Elizabeth asked.

"Yes, it is," Günter replied.

"It's so beautiful and romantic," she said.

"Come on humans, I want to get to Favelyn before the night comes. These are dark times and bad things have been happening in the night."

Nobody disagreed with Günter and they set out through the remainder of the clearing. They slowly made their way into the forest. The canopy was extremely dense and only rays of sunlight broke through making a dim light. There weren't any trails in this forest and one could easily get lost without the proper guide.

The dwarf reached into a pouch and produced three sets of wire-rimmed glasses. He handed a pair to both Jacob and Elizabeth.

The frames had no lenses in them and were mangled beyond repair. On the end of the temple tips of the frames were small amethyst crystals.

"What are these for, Günter?" Jacob asked.

"They've been enchanted with the ability to see the trails leading into Favelyn," Günter told them.

"Where did you get these little gems?" Elizabeth asked.

"Don't you worry about that," he told her, "and they better not find a way into your pockets when we get there."

"Don't you worry about that," Jacob said mimicking him. "We have a little more scruples than that."

"Very funny, just make sure you have my gold ready when we get there," Günter grumbled and trudged off into the forest.

"Be nice," Elizabeth said and slipped her glasses on. The forest took on a new form. Even the trees looked different. These trees were old and ancient relics of times past. A well-groomed path set out before them, curving into the forest and out of sight. In the distance she could make out pixies and fairies dancing through the air around the trees.

"Fairies," Elizabeth said in surprise.

“Really,” Jacob said quickly putting on his glasses and looking in the direction she was gazing.

“Mind yourself,” Günter told them, “and stay on the trail. Fairies and pixies may look pretty but they are nasty little creatures.”

“So are dwarfs,” Jacob mumbled.

“Really now,” Elizabeth said, turning towards him, “are you not an adult?”

“Well, he started it,” Jacob complained, “with his human comments.”

Elizabeth just shook her head and followed Günter down the path. Although the forest was beautiful they could feel a heaviness around them. Something was smothering the life out in this place. They travelled on wooden bridges, over majestic streams racing down the mountain, but still the life was gone.

“What has happened here?” Elizabeth asked.

“The elves do not leave their city,” Günter told her. “They’re the life and blood of this forest and without them tending it, the forest will surely die.”

“That’s horrible!” she responded.

The group came around a bend and they were stopped by a small contingent of armed elven guards. The dwarf ducked behind

Elizabeth. Jacob walked up to the guard standing in front of the group. He felt Günter tug on his pants as he passed by him.

"I think you owe me something," he told Jacob.

"Of course, you're right," Jacob told him.

"Pay the dwarf please," one of the guards told him, "so he'll leave."

Jacob pulled a small pouch of gold coins from his cargo pants pocket and tossed it to the dwarf. Günter opened it up and took a deep breath in through his large nose. A large toothy grin filled his face.

"I love the smell of gold in the morning," he snorted and quickly left the area. Once he got a safe distance from the elves he let out a sigh of relief. He never liked dealing with elves. They were too clean. Just then he realized that he forgot his glasses but decided that a pouch of gold this big could easily replace them.

"Thank you for such a pleasant trip through the mines," Elizabeth called out to him. The group watched as Günter made his way back into the woods in the direction of the caves.

"Well then," Jacob said, turning towards the guard that talked earlier. "Adelwyn, it is good to see you again. What brings you out from the court?"

"Grave news," Adelwyn told them.

“What happened?” Elizabeth asked.

“There has been another murder and this time it strikes close to home. When the royal guard went to prepare the chamber for the hearings, they found Arion dead,” Adelwyn said with darkness in his voice.

“Oh dear,” Elizabeth said, knowing that Arion was Adelwyn’s uncle.

“He was beheaded,” the elf added. Elizabeth immediately gasped and put a hand to her mouth. Ignoring customs she hugged Adelwyn while she grieved for him.

“Who did it?” Jacob asked.

“Blood elves,” Adelwyn said pulling back from Elizabeth. “Arion killed one during the struggle. Then two more were caught at the city border trying to escape through a fire route.

“A fire route?” Elizabeth said inquisitively. “That means the Dark Elves are also involved.”

“Exactly,” Adelwyn said, confirming her thoughts.

“I hate to ask this,” Jacob said, “but with the troubled times, I must ask. Will there still be hearings at a different time?”

"Yes, there will be hearings, but a hearing of a different kind. We called for Dark Elf representation and Adgar himself fire-jumped to Favelyn."

"Isn't he the elder to the Dark Elf clan?" Jacob asked.

"Yes," Adelwyn said, "and then he was arrested by my father's imperial guard. He's being held by the Golden Elves on charges of murder. Just minutes after the arrest, as if they were expecting it to happen, we received a message from the royal courier."

"What did it say?" Jacob asked.

"We have three full moons to release Adgar and if not, then we have declared war."

"What will you do?" Elizabeth asked.

"It's not up to me," he responded, "my father and the other elders will meet to decide."

"What do we do now?" Jacob asked.

"I've been told to get you out of here safely. The last thing we need is the Golden Arrows angry with us for your deaths. We'll protect you all the way back to your house."

***

Norman and his team were long gone by the time the *Mist Traveler* reached the side of the lead transport pod. Arthur and Coulter stood waiting for the crews from both vessels to finish tying off. They could see Lady Meara standing on the deck of her ship shouting orders to her crew. Ropes were being thrown across from ship to ship as they tied the ships together to stabilize the movements of the ships. And this kept them from drifting away from each other. As soon as the crews were done and they placed a plank connecting the two boats, Arthur and Coulter made their way over to Lady Meara. When they crossed over to the water elves' ship they met up with Noah and he guided them to Lady Meara.

"How's everything going, Noah?" Arthur asked.

"Things are not well, my friend. It seems like a war may be brewing in the elven nations."

"Have you heard anything about Jacob and Liz? Are they well?"

"Adelwyn went to Heidelberg to meet with them. Just for a little extra protection until they met up with their guide," he told him.

"Do you know who they got to guide them through the Alps?"

"Yes, the Golden Elves sent a message to them telling them to meet with their old acquaintance Günter and he would guide them. They believed that their mission was compromised and he would be their safest bet."

"Hah," Arthur laughed, "Günter Grendlehook, huh? Elizabeth always had a soft spot for that little crook. You said that Adelwyn was added protection, have things really gotten that bad already?"

"Yes, there have been some attacks on humans by the Blood Elves in the Black Forest region," Noah told him, "but we haven't heard any more news yet."

"We had an attack by a blood elf on the transport pod," Arthur told Noah. They finally made their way through the crew working diligently on the decks and were walking up stairs leading to the bridge where Meara was standing. She had a smile that reached from one ear to the other. Arthur always felt some joy when he saw Lady Meara.

"What's this that I overheard you saying?" she asked Arthur, "There was a blood elf attack on your transport pod?"

"Yes, there was," Coulter answered stoically, "he evaded our capture or he would be sitting in front of us in chains as we speak."

"What happened?" she continued.

"It attacked two of the pod's engineers and then it went after Norman," Arthur told her.

"Oh my goodness!" she gasped. "Is he hurt?"

"No, actually he fought back and knocked the beast down with a blast rod," he told her.

"Of course he did, I knew that boy was something special," she said with the smile returning, "Maybe even something of legends. Where is my little arrow of light?"

"He's doing a special errand for the Matron of the Seas, but he was definitely looking forward to seeing you again. And I told him that I would let you know."

"I was hoping to see his face again before we went after Mordecai, I'll just have to look forward to our next meeting."

"I'm sure he is hoping for the same."

"Do we have a plan for a diversion yet, Arthur?" Meara asked.

"It depends on how many ships we have at our disposal," Coulter intervened.

"Well, you shall have the *Mist Traveler* of course, the Golden Arrow's surveillance boat the *Arrow*, and my brother is piloting the *Sandra Gale* to us right at this minute. Last time I heard from him he was approximately five hours from this point. Whether or not the *Sandra Gale* joins us in our fight is up to Arthur of course," she said.

"Don't kid yourself! The *Sandra Gale* would not miss this fight, so she'll be joining in the diversion. I won't let anything happen to Norman."

"I figured so," Coulter said. "In that case we will have the *Arrow* stay about a mile or so behind us. We'll arrive in a two waves, making Mordecai split his forces. The transport pod will remain under the surface of the water, staying invisible to their view. As Mordecai's men come out after us, the pods will surface and hopefully destroy some vessels," Coulter animated the entire speech with hand gestures and wide arm movements. The other three just stood listening to his instructions, with stern looks on their faces. The situation seemed to be getting darker and darker by the moment. After he was certain that Coulter was done speaking, Arthur turned and scanned the horizon looking for his ship. He would never let the others know but he missed the feel of the *Sandra Gale* beneath his feet and to top that off he'd just sent his nephew into the lion's den. Sensing that something was bothering him, Meara reached out and gently touched his shoulder.

"Is everything all right, Arthur?" she asked him. "You seem troubled and burdened with heavy thoughts."

"I worry about Norman, he's just a young boy, and has not seen the evils he may be facing when he arrives at Mordecai's stronghold."

"Don't worry," interrupted Coulter, "Norman is in good hands with Milton and the royal guard."

"I know that he's in good hands, but he was entrusted to me and now I have no control over his fate. That is why the *Sandra Gale* will do her part in this mission."

"You've every right to worry," Meara told him, "it's not like he is being protected by the imperial elven army," she added with a smirk.

"Excuse me," Coulter said, raising an eyebrow at Meara.

"Come on, Coulter. Everyone knows that the safest place in the world is being surrounded by the imperial elven army," she laughed out loud. Arthur looked from her to Coulter and joined in with her laughter. His spirits were lifted a little by the laughter with friends.

Chapter Twenty Nine

Norman and the Myhr arrived just outside the inner harbor of Mordecai's stronghold. Everyone let go of their dolphins and Milton gave them some hand gestures, then the dolphins swam off away from the area. Norman just floated in the water trying to get his bearings. It was a wild ride on the dolphin gliders.

"What are we doing now?" Norman asked Milton.

"We are waiting to make contact with Arthur."

"He'll be able to communicate with us?"

"Yes, he'll be able to." Milton gestured toward the other Myhr, "I want two of you to swim ahead and find the flood pipes on the southern side of the inner harbor."

A couple of the Myhr swam off towards the inner harbor. Norman was amazed at how fast they could swim. Their hands and feet were webbed, which helped propel them through the water at incredible speeds.

"Now we just wait," Milton said.

***

Three boats made their way towards the stronghold, a very small but impressive fleet. In the lead was Arthur's pride and joy the *Sandra Gale*, a research vessel with a lot of surprises in her still. Just behind her was the elves' wooden warship the *Mist Traveler*, and about a football field back from them was the *Arrow*. It was the Golden Arrows' premier surveillance boat. It may just look like an old fishing trawler, but it was loaded with the world's best spy gear and some the world doesn't even know about.

The captain of the *Arrow* was a good friend of Arthur and a lead hunter for Golden Arrows, Fuller Smithouse. His friends call him 'Coach' for some reason, but the story has never come out.

"Arthur," Coach called out over the radio, "do you know what we are up against?"

"I'm not totally sure but I wouldn't put anything past Mordecai."

"Is it true that you had a run-in with a blood elf?"

"It wasn't me, actually. It was my nephew, Norman"

"Jacob's Norman?"

"The one and only," he said, "and don't get started on this arrow of light stuff, the kid has enough to worry about without adding that burden on him."

"I didn't say anything," Coach defended himself, "but the prophecy talked of one hundred and twenty six signs that would be present the year of his birth. If I recall properly they were all present the year of his birth. Not to mention he was the only child born that year in the whole League of Golden Arrows."

"I'm not disputing the facts. I just don't want him to worry about proving something to everyone."

"I understand," Coach told him.

The *Arrow* increased it speed to pull up next to the *Mist Traveler* so it could communicate with them. The elves' boat did not have modern communication gear on it; they still communicated with the nautical flag system. The engines on the trawler were pretty strong and within no time the boats were side by side.

The *Arrow* pulled to the starboard side of the *Mist Traveler*. Noah was already waiting for them. Coach was letting the new recruit drive the boat while he went out to talk to Noah.

"Don't hit them," Coach said as he walked outside. The kid gave him a nervous look.

Coach stood at the portside of his boat while the two pulled closer. *Not too close,* he thought to himself again. Noah shook his head as he saw the well-known Golden Arrow getting closer. He smiled and waved at Coach.

"Why do you have those silly flags in your hands?" Noah yelled to him.

"So we can communicate," he yelled back.

"We are talking right now, aren't we?"

"Yes," Coach said, dropping the flags to the deck of his boat.

"So what does all your fancy gear tell us about Mordecai's stronghold?"

"It actually doesn't show much activity. We do have some satellite pictures of boats anchored in the inner harbor. Unfortunately, it's a working harbor. So it could just be their boats."

"What news do you have for us then?"

"I've received a message from our headquarters in Edinburgh," he told Noah, "the hearings in the royal court have been cancelled."

"What! Are you sure?" Noah asked him.

"I'm positive. I called on the satellite phone after the report came through to actually talk to someone."

"What happened? They have never cancelled a hearing before."

"I am sorry to tell you this, but Arion has been murdered."

"No!" Noah gasped out in utter shock and disbelief.

“They believe it was the Dark Elves, they captured two blood elves trying to escape through a fire jump and one was killed by Arion at the scene of the murder.”

“This can’t be!” Noah said. He was still unable to bring himself to believing this could happen. “I must go talk to Lady Meara, I will return shortly.”

“Hold on,” Coach called out, “there is more. Adgar has been arrested by the Golden Elves and the Dark Elves are threatening war if he is not released.”

Noah didn’t even respond, he just turned and walked back to the bridge, where Lady Meara was piloting the ship. Coach could see him gesture for her to walk off to the side where they could talk in private. After a short while he could see the obvious reaction to the news. Her knees buckled a little, and her hands went to her mouth while her head just shook from side to side in disbelief. She looked back over at Coach then back to Noah again. They seemed to talk for a while more before Noah made his way back to the starboard railing. His eyes were moist.

“Lady Meara said that we’ll finish the mission, departing immediately after the completion. We may not even say good-bye,” Noah told him.

“I understand,” Couch responded. “We’ll be ready to start the diversion in five minutes, just wait for Arthur to blow his horn. That’s the signal to move in and attack. This will give Milton and Norman the opportunity to get in and get the Maiden."

"Okay."

***

"Norman or Milton, are you guys there?" Arthur's voice came through the helmet's speakers.

"We're here," Milton responded.

"We're on station as well," Arthur said, "I'll give you ten minutes, then we'll start the diversion."

"That sounds good," Milton said.

"Norman, how are you doing?"

"Uncle Arthur, I rode on a dolphin. Could it get any better than this?"

"All right, you guys get going and we'll start the diversion up here in ten minutes. Good luck, everyone."

"You too," Milton said. "Norman grab onto my shoulders. It will be easier for you to keep up with us." Norman swam over and grabbed onto Milton's shoulders and they were off. He didn't know who swam faster, the dolphins or the Myhr, it was very close. Arthur's voice echoed in Norman's head as they swam off. He was really enjoying this summer with his uncle.

Chapter Thirty

When the group arrived at the flood pipes, they met up with the first two that swam ahead. One of the two Myhr held out a stick about two feet in length with a 'C' at the end of it. A yellow-orange beam stretched between the tips of the 'C' and they were cutting through the grate that covered the pipes entrance.

"What's that?" Norman asked.

"It's a plasma cutter," Milton told him, "it can burn in water and those bars are no problem for it."

The plasma cutter was getting the job done, but it wasn't moving at the fastest pace. Norman kept scanning the waters nearby for anything or anyone lurking around. Norman would be tapping his foot on the ground if he could. He was busy trying to keep himself level with the entrance of the pipe and they just finished cutting through the third pipe. This seemed to be taking forever.

"How much longer do you think it'll take?" Norman asked Milton.

"We're moving as fast as the cutter will go."

"Are there sharks that will come in this close?"

“I wish I could tell you no, but there are sharks that will come into the harbor,” Milton told him. This made Norman a little nervous and he started to look everywhere for sharks. He didn’t see any but he did see a large amount of boats floating on the surface.

“What are those boats doing there?” Norman asked.

“What boats?” Milton asked Norman.

“Up there,” Norman responded, pointing to the surface, “it looks like there are twenty or thirty of them.”

“Oh no! I think it’s a trap,” Milton said as the boats started to move from the harbor to intercept Arthur and the others.

“Arthur, can you hear me?” he called out to the team but there was no answer.

***

Mordecai stood on the balcony in front of the railing, watching the inevitable defeat of his arch enemy, Arthur Skylair. He couldn’t take his eyes off the *Sandra Gale*; an evil grin crossed his face. James walked out of the control room and stood by his side.

“Sir, what is the next move you would like to make?”

“Open the gates and release them. There will most likely be someone trying to get in through the bottom.”

“How do you know they’ll be there?”

"It's what I would have done, and Arthur is almost as smart as me."

"I'll go and pull the lever myself."

"Hurry, and then I want you take the lead to intercept the *Sandra Gale*."

"I will."

"Oh yeah, Mr. James?"

"Yes."

"I don't want Arthur escaping this time."

"Of course, sir, I'll do it myself."

James departed quickly from his boss and ran down to the lower levels where he could open the gates.

***

"Almost there," said the Myhr that was cutting through the grates that covered the pipe's entrance.

"What's that noise?" Milton asked.

"I don't know, but I hear it too," Norman told him.

A loud clicking sound was coming from their right. It sounded like it was resonating from the inside of the cliff wall itself. They all looked around to see where it might be coming from and that's when they saw their worst fears. Some kind of shaft was opened up and three medium-sized tiger sharks came bursting out into the open.

"Not again," Norman sighed.

"Done," the Myhr exclaimed. The metal grate to the pipe fell down the side of the cliff to the sea floor. The sharks turned towards the commotion of the grill and started to swim towards them.

"Norman, get into the pipe now. You must get to the Maiden."

Norman, Milton, and two of the other Myhr swam into the pipe quickly. As soon as Norman was in he turned to look at the other teammates, but they were nowhere to be seen. Norman started to swim back but Milton grabbed his shoulder.

"No, Norman! They are leading the sharks away so we can finish the mission."

"What do you think will happen to them, will they be hurt?"

"I hope not, Norman, but they do it so we can rescue the Maiden. They'll risk their lives to make sure she is safe. So we must move on and get her."

"Okay."

Norman turned around and swam deeper into the pipe with the rest of the team. The pipe was about ten feet in diameter and had plenty of room for the group of four. Milton led the way with Norman behind him and the other two taking up the rear.

"Where are we going, Milton?"

"Look in the far corner of your visor."

"All right, there is some kind of blinking light."

"That's where we believe they are keeping the Maiden, so we must make our way towards her."

They swam on for what seemed like ages. The pipe started to narrow as they got further in. Norman looked above him and saw another grill in the piping; it had a latch holding it up. It was very small in comparison to the pipe they were already in.

"Should we be going through that pipe above us?"

"I think that you are the only one that can fit into it, and we're not going to separate."

"I agree."

"So for now you stay with us and we move forward. We are coming up alongside the Maiden and we need to prepare to break through the wall."

After another twenty feet of swimming they stopped and Milton went up to the wall, feeling around for something to open it up with, maybe a latch or an opening in the pipe. After a few seconds of searching he waved one of the other Myhr over to him and pointed to four places on the wall. Norman watched as the Myhr placed four small things on the wall. One was placed on top of the other and the other two were placed off to either side of them. They resembled orange putty, and then they placed a small rod in each one with a wire coming from them.

"Wait a minute," Norman called out, "I've seen this in movies. Is this going to explode?"

"Yes it is, Norman."

"Are we going to get hurt?"

"No, they're designed to explode into the rock and away from us. You just have to be careful when the water rushes into the tunnel to fill the hole, it will create a vortex and suck you in."

Norman held his breath as he watched the Myhr swim back a couple of feet from the wall. He put his hands to his ears to try and block the noise. The one with the detonator turned and looked to make sure everyone was a safe distance away. Norman watched his finger move in slow motion as he compressed the trigger. Norman felt a thud hit him in the chest and he was pushed back a couple of feet. Then he watched as the stone on the inside of the pipe exploded into a hallway on the opposite side. Suddenly, he was being pulled through the large opening that it made in the wall.

Chapter Thirty One

Arthur stood on the bridge of the *Sandra Gale* as what looked like thirty boats raced out towards him. They were loaded with men and large guns mounted to a few of the boats. He smiled and pushed the throttle forward, getting everything that he could from his engines. The large research vessel bounded forward towards them.

"For Norman!" Arthur bellowed out.

The boats split up and raced around the *Sandra Gale,* almost hitting each other as they came around the back of the boat. Arthur spun around to look out the aft windows to see what happened. He could see the men on the boats regaining their composure and they started to man the mounted guns.

"Uh-oh," Arthur gasped.

He turned to the helm of the ship and spun the wheel causing the boat to lurch towards the portside. The front end of the *Sandra Gale* rose up about twenty feet out of the water and came down throwing water in all directions. Arthur could hear the shots fired from the large gun, but with his maneuvering the bullets fell short of their intended target. Unfortunately, he didn't believe that they would miss him again with the next round of bullets. Once the boat settled into its new direction it began to pick speed back up again. He just had to get them to follow him a little bit longer.

The *Mist Traveler* was not as lucky as the *Sandra Gale*. The old wooden boat could not maneuver like the small boats racing around her. Her sails were ripped to shreds and the wood was littered with bullet holes and shrapnel. The *Mist Traveler* was badly wounded.

The *Arrow* stayed back in the distance, keeping in communication with the transport pod beneath the waves. Arthur had turned his boat to lead the enemy away from the stronghold, giving Norman and the team a better chance.

"Coutler, are you standing by?" Couch called down to the Myhr.

"We are," he responded.

"Perfect, when you surface, aim for the largest group. There are about twenty boats in pursuit of Arthur."

***

James led the attack in the largest boat. He was trying to shout orders over the sound of all the commotion. Water was spraying in their faces as the boat leaped over the wake that the *Sandra Gale* made.

"You there, get on the fifty caliber and put some lead on that target," he yelled to the nearest person.

"All right."

The man was the perfect fit for the job. He looked to be well over six feet tall and about two-hundred-eighty pounds of pure muscle. He was covered in tattoos and had a nasty looking Fu Manchu mustache. His right eye had a large scar that started above his eye and went down through it to the middle of his cheek. The man grabbed the gun and pulled back the lever loading the chain of bullets into the chamber.

"Don't miss this time like those idiots in the other boat," James commanded him.

"I won't," he told him, "that captain is as good as dead."

The man used his one good eye to lock onto the *Sandra Gale* through the cross hairs. It was difficult with the person driving the boat over every wave it could possibly jump. The man breathed in deeply and steadied himself for the shot.

The *Sandra Gale* shook as she pushed forward trying to avoid all the boats coming up on either side of her. Arthur wiped his sweaty brow on his shirt sleeve and smiled as he steered, concentrating on a certain point in the water ahead of him. He didn't even notice all of the bullets hitting his boat or the smoke pouring out of different areas on the boat. He could see a large shadow forming under the water, but he doubted that his chasers would notice what was happening before it was too late. He pushed the throttles as hard as he could, trying to squeeze out every drop of power in the engine room.

Before he heard the glass in the porthole shatter he felt the fire burning through his shoulder as the immensely large bullet tore through the outer portion of his right shoulder. It caused him to spin towards the right and slam into the bulkhead of the bridge. Luckily he let go of the wheel as he flew through the air. He landed with a thud and could barely remain awake as he stared out of the front window where he could see the huge shadow underneath the surface of the water. Soon his boat was roaring over it and a large smile spread across his face.

The large man with the scar on his face was too preoccupied with the shot he just made. He didn't realize they were being led into a trap until it was too late. He stared with horror as he saw half of the other boats full of mercenaries being thrown into the air as a huge submarine surfaced beneath them. The people onboard were flung in every direction as they plummeted back into the ocean waters.

The rest of the boats were being attacked by some monsters from the deep. They looked like mutated lobsters and crabs. There was a woman and a man standing on the back of a huge whale calling out commands to the monsters.

"Turn the boat," James shouted.

The helmsman spun the boat hard to port, causing the boat to jerk and bounce, throwing one of the men out into the water. He threw the throttle forward and tried to out run the monsters, but to little avail. The Crusteans crawled over the sides and ripped the boat and the crew to shreds.

The large pod was completely out of the water now and Myhr were swarming out of it and jumping into the water. The mercenaries were no match and easily over taken by the Myhr and Crusteans. The two races fought together like they were brothers.

Coulter stared in amazement as the Crusteans fought on the Maiden's behalf. He couldn't understand what had just happened. The two were sworn enemies, but now they're fighting together. Michael and Crystal continued on towards the stronghold, riding on the back of their whale. Mullick climbed onto the back of the whale and joined the chase.

Arthur slid himself across the floor to the controls on the bridge. He grabbed onto the console and pulled himself up, steadying himself by leaning on the console. His right shoulder throbbed in pain but he was able to move it and that relieved him a bit. He pulled back on the throttle, slowing the *Sandra Gale* down eventually to a stop. Smoke was pouring out of different sections of the boat and he needed to make sure the fires were put out.

Mordecai stood on the balcony as he watched with both horror and delight. He was pleased to see the *Sandra Gale* limping away with smoke bellowing from it. On the other hand, he wondered what was to become of his men that he sent out there. Although, he really didn't care, he just wondered. He let out a small laugh and turned to make his way down to the Maiden. As he walked towards the door that would lead him downstairs, he was suddenly thrown to the floor by a large explosion that shook the foundation of the entire facility. The room went dark immediately as they lost power, but was soon illuminated by the emergency lighting that came on quickly. The flood lights combined with the smoke and dust put out an eerie glow throughout the rooms. Mordecai pushed himself up to his feet and tried to shake out the ringing that was going through his head right that minute. Already knowing what was happening, he made his way to his office to arm himself.

Chapter Thirty Two

Norman stood in front of the glass prison that held the Maiden and raised his hand, pressing it against the window. His hand started to glow blue as he got it closer to the Maiden. She instantly moved towards him and placed her hand over his on her side of the glass, but nothing happened when she put it on the glass. There was no warm magical feeling that Norman thought he might have transferring the power to her. Nothing seemed to happen.

"Norman," Milton called out to him, "I don't think you can do the transfer through the glass. I think you need to break it."

"How can I do that?"

"Use the blast rod, the one that your uncle gave you."

"Oh, yeah!"

"Pull it out and shatter that glass and do it quickly, the water is beginning to rise."

Norman looked at Milton then turned his head back to the Maiden. The water was already up to his waist and rising quickly. He pulled his bag off of his shoulder and reached into it, pulling out the blast rod.

“Stand back!” he shouted to the Maiden. She ran to the other side of the room and turned her face away from the window. He raised his hand up into the air and was about to slam the rod into the window when a huge wall of water came up between him and the window.

“I wouldn’t do that if I were you,” Mordecai shouted above the sound of rushing water. Everyone turned to see Mordecai with his hand extended out in front of him, controlling the water. On his hand was a gold ring with a large glowing red gem in the shape of a skull on it. He moved his hand across the front of his body, quickly causing the water wall to slam the four of them to the other side of the room. Norman was thrown back through the hole in the wall while he watched the others hit the wall surrounding the hole.

“Stay where you are, Norman,” he heard Milton’s voice in his helmet.

“I need to help you rescue the Maiden,” Norman called out as he tried to swim against the current.

“Let us fight him before you come back in,” Milton insisted.

Norman didn’t know what to do. He had to fight to keep himself from being pulled back into the room from the strong current of water rushing in. He decided to swim back about ten feet away from the hole and see if that was any better. As he got away from the strongest part of the current he noticed the small grate at the side of the pipe he was in. He was wondering where it led to, when it dawned on him and he remembered seeing a drain on the side of the Maiden's wall in her prison. He swam over to it and tried to pull it off, but his attempts were useless. He couldn't budge the grate with his hands. That's when he saw the blast rod lying on the bottom of the pipe. He must have dropped it when he was thrown into there by Mordecai. He swam down and grabbed it, then pushed off the bottom and thrust himself to the grate.

He took a deep breath and slammed the rod into the grate. It blew inward with a fury and he could hear the metal grate smacking against the inside of the pipe that led off the main pipe. He peered into the darkness of the pipe; he could see about nine feet in and he noticed that he would just be able to fit. He could only go forward or backwards, the space was too tight to turn around and swim out. He would have to back out.

"This isn't normal," he said to himself as he shook off his fears and swam into the hole. He kept his arms stretched out in front of him. He was still holding the blast rod while he slowly kicked his way through the pipe. It felt like the walls of the pipe were closing in around him.

"Norman, where are you?" Milton called out.

"I'm in a pipe," Norman responded, "I think that it will lead me to the Maiden."

"Are you sure about this?"

“I have a feeling,” was all Norman could think of saying to him.

“Follow your instincts, Norman, but be safe.”

“Are you guys okay?” Norman asked.

“One of my men is hurt badly, but he will be okay. I am going after Mordecai and the other two are looking after the Maiden’s cousin.”

Norman seemed to swim forward with a little more determination now. It was up to him to save the Maiden. All of the others were busy fighting their own battles. As he swam for what seemed like forever, he finally came to the metal drain that he believed was on the wall to the Maiden’s room. He didn’t even wait to contemplate it. He thrust his hand holding the blast rod forward and struck the rod into the metal plate. It blew out into the room and for a brief second Norman could see into the Maiden’s chamber, then he was shot out of the pipe like a bullet from all the water rushing out from behind him and around him. He slid across the floor of the room like a waterslide at a theme park. Trying to stand up he slipped, from the water still pouring into the room from the pipe, and landed right on the ground. When he looked up he saw the Maiden’s hand out stretched to him, so he grabbed it and she helped him to his feet. The moment she touched his skin he couldn’t feel anything happening. He should have felt the power that was given to him surging out of his body. *Something is wrong,* he thought to himself.

"Is something wrong?" she asked him.

"Yes, I'm supposed to give you something," Norman told her.

"What are you supposed to give me?" she asked.

"The Matron gave me some power that I was to give you, but it didn't happen. Wait a minute, where's your birthmark?"

"It is on my shoulder, why do you need to know?"

"I need to see it, hurry!"

"I don't understand," she said as she slightly turned to show him her birthmark.

Norman reached forward. "This is from the Matron of the Seas," he said as he touched the birthmark with his finger. Energy surged from his finger tip into her body, causing her eyes to roll up and her body to shake. Norman could physically feel the energy being drained from his body. When the transfer was done they both sat there motionless for a minute or two.

They were jolted back to reality when the water started to touch their chins. It was rising quicker than they could react, within seconds it was over their heads. Norman pointed towards the window. She nodded and gestured for him to back up. Her arms moved forward very quickly and a rush of water slammed into the glass breaking through it with ease. They both swam out into the hallway that was already flooded. They both looked around for a way out and then

Norman noticed the stairs leading up. He swam to them and she followed him. Eventually both of them came to the top of the rising waters.

After going up the stairs they came to the large room that housed the wall of monitors. They could see the ocean and the *Sandra Gale* outside of all the windows. Norman saw Milton staggering down the balcony that was outside of the windows. The two of them ran for the door that led outside. When they made it out to him, Norman noticed that he was injured and had blood running down the side of his face. Milton looked up at Norman and the Maiden with terror in his eyes.

"Norman, it's a trap," he tried to tell them, but it was too late. Mordecai lifted his arm over his head and a huge wave crashed down into the balcony, hitting Norman and the others. He slid across the balcony and grabbed onto the railing as his feet swung off over the edge.

"I'm getting sick of being thrown around by water," Norman thought to himself. He looked over and saw the Maiden and Milton down in the water below. He tried to pull himself up onto the balcony but Mordecai appeared above him. He reached down and grabbed ahold of Norman, pulling him up onto the balcony with him.

"Who are you?"

"My name is Norman."

Mordecai looked at the boy then back out at the *Sandra Gale* again. Suddenly he realized who was sitting on the ground in front of him. Mordecai cackled an evil laugh, one that Norman was sure he would never forget.

"I should have known, you look just like your father Jacob. So you're the boy, the legendary arrow of light. The prophecy says that you will usher in a time of peace. Hah…watch me, Norman Skylair, as I destroy your uncle's ship and him with it."

Mordecai raised his hand high into the air and started to bring forth a huge wave to crush the *Sandra Gale*. Norman kicked his foot into Mordecai's left knee, trying to stop him from hurting his uncle. Mordecai buckled and he fell to one knee. He glared at Norman as he stood back up.

"Norman Skylair, you are about to join in your uncle's fate," he said, pointing his hand at Norman, "and that will be the end of your era of peace."

Norman tried to crawl away from him, but Mordecai grabbed his ankles and picked him up. All Norman saw was the ground disappear and be replaced by the ocean as Mordecai hung him out over the railing. Norman's heart started to race and the blood was running to his head.

"Time for you to leave," Mordecai roared.

Mordecai let go of Norman's ankles. Time seemed to move in slow motion for Norman as he passed the first railing. He flailed both arms out as the second rail passed by and hooked his arm into the railing. It caused him to whip around and lose his hold on the second railing, but since his descent was slowed he was able to grab onto the last railing. He dangled there in pain looking up at the man that would inevitably kick him into the water. Mordecai stood there, trying to catch his breath, as he continued to glare at Norman.

"That was pretty amazing, but it was your last move," Mordecai snarled.

"I got one more," Norman said as he swung the blasting rod straight up into the bottom of the balcony. Cement and railing flew in every direction. Mordecai launched against the wall and then fell into the sea. Norman just let go as he hit the stone and fell straight down into the water. Norman looked up as stones started to fall down towards him. He felt the pain as some of them hit him but didn't injure him too badly. Then Norman felt himself being pulled out of the water by the collar of his clothes.

He looked up to see who was saving him and it was an old man with leather skin. He was wearing a weathered fisherman's coat. Norman remembered the old man from the scrimshaw shop in Newport. It was Morton. It was at that moment that Norman realized that he also saved Mordecai.

"Why would you save him?"

“No one deserves to die, Norman, and besides, he’s my friend.”

Morton picked up the limp body of Mordecai and threw him over his shoulders. The old man carried him up the rocky embankment and turned back to Norman. Norman could see the same look in Morton’s eyes that he saw with Mordecai.

“Norman, just remember this. My debt to your mother is repaid in full. If we meet again we will be enemies.” And with that Morton turned and disappeared over the rocks. Norman just sat there half in the water and half on the rocks. He saw the glitter of something shiny sitting on the rock just a few inches from the top of the water. He reached over to pick it up and realized it was the ring that Mordecai was wearing.

Norman turned and looked out towards the bay. He saw Michael and Crystal riding towards him on what looked like a whale. He felt good just to see the two of them and even Mullick riding behind them was a nice surprise. As they got closer Mullick jumped off and disappeared under the water only to reappear ten feet from Norman. He lifted Norman carefully, making sure not to hurt him, and carried him back to the whale.

“Welcome to my whale,” Michael said, looking back at Norman. He just laughed as the whale carried him back to his uncle’s ship.

Chapter Thirty Three

Elizabeth sat staring out the window of the plane as it flew through the clouds. Everything was so tense since they left Germany. They were whisked out under the cover of night. There wasn't even a break from the meeting with Adelwyn until they got on the plane. Jacob plopped into the seat next to her.

"Stop fooling around, Jacob!"

"What did I do?" he asked, trying not to spill the glass of water he just got. She just turned and looked back out the window.

"Life has just gotten too serious in an instant," she said, "and I don't like it one bit!"

"Soon we will be back in Florida and everything can go back to normal for us."

"What do you mean? Do you really think that this will just fade away into the shadows?"

"No, but the high council has already said that they will be getting involved personally to help stop any war."

The back door of the cabin swung open and a tall forest elf named Eric came through it carrying a short, fat and hairy dwarf. The dwarf was not coming willingly, he was kicking and squirming and spouting off some colorful adjectives. Eric dropped Günter into the seat across from Jacob, which was quite a drop due to the difference in height between a dwarf and Eric.

"We have a stowaway," Eric said, not even looking at Günter.

"What are you doing here?" Jacob asked.

"Are you kidding me?" Günter pleaded. "You would be crazy to stay in the Black Forest. Bloodshed is going to erupt at any moment."

At that moment the pilot came out of the front cabin to see what all the commotion was. He took one look at Günter and just shook his head.

"Give me a reason why I shouldn't launch you out of the back hatch, and it better be a good one, dwarf," the pilot informed him.

"Information," was all that Günter said.

"What information?" Elizabeth asked him.

"First you have to agree to let me stay."

"That depends, dwarf," the captain interjected, "on whether or not it's good information."

"Fair enough," Günter said, and he looked around the cabin to make sure he had everyone's attention. "We are being followed."

"Followed?" said Jacob.

"Yes, we are being followed. I saw it out the window in the aft cabin."

"What did you see?" asked Elizabeth.

"A shadow dragon!"

"Nonsense," Eric laughed.

"It's true, I saw it with my own eyes. He's moving through the dark sides of the clouds."

"I'll go and see for myself." The captain said, "and if you are lying, then out the door you go," the captain left them in the inner cabin then went aft to look for the dragon. They all waited patiently for the captain's return. Eric nudged the dwarf.

"Are you nervous?" he asked the dwarf.

"No, I'm not," Günter said, "I know what I saw."

The captain came through the cabin quickly, calling out to the co-pilot. Everyone jumped at the urgency in his voice.

"At the first break in the clouds, move up above them," he called to the co-pilot.

"Was it a shadow dragon?" Elizabeth asked.

“Unfortunately, it was, and we must get going. I don’t know who would summon a shadow dragon, but they must intend to hurt someone.”

“What do you mean who?” Günter said. “It has to be the Dark Elves of course.”

“How do you know?” Jacob asked.

“No one else could accomplish that kind of powerful dark magic.”

The pilot left the group and headed up front. He closed the door and turned on the light, telling them to sit down and put their buckles on. Once again everything was tense. After a few minutes of silence the plane pulled up hard to get above the clouds.

***

Fayne stood in front of an empty store room in the back of the Tattered Spine. It was not completely empty. Unfortunately, the scrolls that he was looking for were not in there. A dark elf enchantress stood quietly off to the side and two soldiers stood next to him. Fayne clenched his fist in disgust. The scrolls seemed to have eluded him again.

“Where’s the shadow dragon?” he asked the enchantress.

“She’s following the plane as you requested,” she told him matter of factly.

"Will they be landing soon?" he demanded.

"Within the hour," one of the soldiers told him.

He turned to face the soldiers and the enchantress. The rage in his face could hardly be controlled. He glanced back at the half empty shelves, then back to the rest.

"We'll be at the house waiting for them," he commanded.

"Yes sir," the soldiers said in unison.

"Make sure that the dragon is there," he added, pointing at the female dark elf.

Chapter Thirty Four

Norman stood on the deck of the *Sandra Gale* as he watched the Maiden of the Seas destroy Mordecai's stronghold with a huge wave. The water ripped through the stone and steel like it was tissue paper. He was actually enjoying watching it. It didn't take long for the waters to completely erase the entire stronghold. The Maiden seemed very satisfied with the devastation to the complex; she took a deep breath, nodded her head and turned back towards Norman.

"Norman and Arthur, I would like to thank you both for all that you have done here."

"You're welcome," was all that Norman said. Arthur just nodded.

The Maiden turned to Arthur, "My father has told me many stories of your adventures with our people. It was exciting to know that I am now part of one of your extraordinary adventures."

"It was my pleasure to assist the people of Myrh once again."

The Maiden walked over to Michael and Crystal. She stopped right in front them. Everybody seemed to hold their breath.

“I was too young to remember the dark times. My father told me horror stories of the Crusteans and what they did to us,” she said.

“Young Maiden, I didn’t even exist at the time of the battle. I was born after and developed a new strain of mutation,” Michael told her.

“We were wrong,” the Maiden said and put out her hand. Michael took it and shook her hand in return.

“It’ll take our people time, but we’ll work on learning to live together in peace. You have my word,” the Maiden told Michael.

“And you have mine as well,” Michael told her.

“Well with everything in the stronghold destroyed, I guess we’ll be leaving then,” the Maiden said, turning back towards the stronghold.

“Oh, wait,” Norman blurted out, “there is still this.”

Norman reached into his pocket and pulled out the ring that Mordecai was using to control the waters of the world and handed it to the Maiden. She took it from him with a look of pain and disgust. Then she turned and handed it to Milton to carry back to the transport pod. She walked over to Norman and leaned over and gave him a hug.

“Good-bye, Norman, until our paths cross again.”

“Good-bye.”

Norman and his uncle stood on the boat and watched as the transport pod made its descent back into the depths of the water. Lady Meara and her crew departed immediately after the battle. Arthur walked up and put his good arm around Norman's shoulders.

"Are you ready to head back home, Norman? Back to the normal world, as you might put it."

"Yes, I am, but could we stop by the Statue of Liberty again if we have time?"

"Of course we can."

Norman followed his uncle up to the bridge and took his seat in the co-pilot's chair. He looked around at the big empty ocean before him. Then he turned his chair to face his uncle.

"It feels kind of lonely now that everyone has gone."

"Do you wish that you could still be on some kind of adventure?"

"Yeah, that would be cool."

"Well, I'll talk to your parents and see if you can spend next summer with me again."

"You would do that for me?'

"Of course I would, Norman. I really enjoyed this summer with you."

"I enjoyed it too, Uncle Arthur."

Arthur pushed the throttle down and started the boat, heading home. The trip back to Florida was very uneventful. They stopped by the Statue of Liberty and a few other harbors between Canada and the *Sandra Gale*'s homeport.

***

The sun was blazing in the afternoon sky when Norman and Arthur pulled into the pier in Sarasota. Norman's heart skipped a beat when he saw his home state again. He didn't even realize that he missed it so much.

"Are we heading back to North Port?" Norman asked.

"Not yet, Norman, last time I talked to your parents they asked that I bring you to the house after supper. They had some affairs that they needed to attend to."

"Some affairs?"

"Yes, they said it was very important."

"Okay."

After mooring the ship to the pier, Norman showered and packed his bags. He just stuffed everything into the bag and zipped it up. Grabbing his bag, he ran up to the top deck and waited for his uncle to join him. They walked down to the pier together and climbed into Uncle Arthur's old green truck. Norman really liked riding in his uncle's truck; it reminded him of an old surfing video he saw a longtime ago. Norman sat there thinking about what it would be like to surf.

"Uncle Arthur, do you think that we could maybe go surfing next summer?"

"I'll see what I can do," he told Norman.

The old truck came to life when he turned the key. They pulled out of the harbor's parking lot and went for dinner at his uncle's favorite Greek restaurant on Main Street. Time seemed to drag while Norman was waiting to get home and see his parents. Finally the bill was paid and they got ready to leave. The sun had set about an hour ago and the moon was shining bright.

Norman sat back and relaxed while the truck drove down the interstate. He was going over the events of the summer in his mind. He couldn't help but smile about the wild time he had with his crazy uncle.

"Uncle Arthur?"

"Yeah, what can I do for you?"

"It feels weird."

"What feels weird, Norman?"

"Well, I had this amazing beginning to my summer and now I'm going to have such a normal life the rest of the summer. It doesn't seem right."

"Life is never normal, Norman, there's always something exciting happening, you just have to pay close attention so you don't miss it when it comes your way."

Talking with his uncle helped pass the time driving home. They were already getting off the highway at his exit. All the signs, stores, and sights were very familiar with Norman and that excitement started to return to his stomach. The only thing different was the new burger joint that was built near the Tattered Spine.

When they turned down the street leading to his house, Norman's heart dropped into his stomach. There were hundreds of red, white, and blue lights flashing in front of his home. As they got closer they could see the flames billowing out of the house. Black smoke was blocking the moonlight out making the scene looking even grimmer.

Norman didn't wait for his uncle to come to a complete stop. As he slowed down, Norman burst out the old truck, tears and all. He made a bee-line for the front door of the house and he would have made it if the firefighter didn't get his arm around his waist. Norman flailed, trying to escape his grip, but the iron hold of the firefighter wouldn't break.

"Where you going, little buddy?"

“That’s my house,” Norman screamed between sobs, “I need to find my parents!”

“You aren’t going in that house, son,” the firefighter declared.

“I need to find my parents,” he sobbed out again.

Arthur finally reached Norman’s side and took him into his arms. He held Norman tight while Norman sobbed into his chest. Arthur guided Norman back to his old truck and put him in the front seat.

“Norman, stay here while I go talk to the officer in charge.”

“I don’t want to.”

“Norman, we’ll talk when I get back. Just give me a few minutes.”

“Okay.”

Norman watched his uncle go talk to some burly police officer. He wanted to get out of the car and run, he didn’t know where he would run but he just wanted to run and hide. He’d come to love and respect his uncle, so he just waited for him to return. Shortly after he left, Arthur returned to the old truck and got into the driver’s seat. He immediately put the car into reverse and started to back out. Norman looked around in every direction.

“Where are we going?” Norman asked.

“We are going to your Aunt Nora’s.”

“Why?”

“I am sorry, Norman, but that is where you’ll have to stay until we can figure something out.”

“What about my parents? What’s wrong with them? Are they…are they…” Norman couldn’t even get it out.

“I don’t know, Norman, the fire chief said that they didn’t find anyone inside.”

“What’s that mean?” he asked.

“I don’t know what it means just yet, Norman,” his uncle said.

Norman started to cry and he put his head to his knees. He didn’t raise it again until he got to his aunt’s house in Sarasota. It was a painful drive.

Chapter Thirty Five

Norman was up in his room packing his green duffle bag. Arthur was here to take him to New York for the Christmas holiday. The remainder of the summer and fall were very long. He thought of his parents every day and almost all day long. Things reminded him of them everywhere he looked. The coded messages that his uncle sent him helped to take his mind off his missing parents. Unfortunately, nothing would ever erase those memories.

He'd stayed with his Aunt Nora since the fire. She was extremely nice and he enjoyed spending time with her. Unfortunately, the house seemed empty since his cousin Lilly left for boarding school. Nora's two youngest girls, his cousins, were fun to be with, but they didn't compare to Lilly.

Arthur was out on the back deck talking with Nora. It was chilly and the two were enjoying some coffee together when Princess Lilliana walked out of the darkness onto the deck. Nora and Arthur were both surprised to see her in America.

"Princess, what are you doing here?" Arthur asked.

"I have urgent matters to talk with you about," she responded.

"When is it not urgent these days?" Nora asked.

“We really need your help, Arthur,” Lilliana said, “and we actually need Norman, too.”

“Why?” Arthur said a little too brusquely.

“Arthur,” she said trying to calm him, “the elven nations are at war.”

“I don’t understand,” Arthur said. “Didn’t the Golden Elves release Adgar like the Dark Elves insisted?”

“They did, but it didn’t help,” she told them. “As soon as he returned to their lands, they declared the Golden Elves an enemy to all the elves.”

“Oh my!” Nora blurted out.

Arthur walked over and sat on the bench on the edge of the deck. He looked out and up at the stars, holding the coffee cup to keep his hands warm. He pursed his lips, deep in thought.

“How can we help you?”

“The treaties,” she told them, “they are being held by the Clockwork Dwarves of Banff Mountain. We need you to go to Banff and acquire the treaties and bring them to Florin.”

“The floating citadel Florin?” Nora asked

“The one and only,” she told them.

"And what about Norman?" Arthur asked Lilliana. "Why do you need him?"

"Many believe that he truly is the 'arrow of light'."

"Come on, Lilliana, there is nothing that has proven that yet. It was just a bunch of silly signs."

"Our people need him now more than ever. Just the mere mention of his existence brings hope."

Norman walked out the back door onto the deck packed and ready to go. He was surprised to see his cousin Lilly standing there. The three of them just stood there looking at Norman, like they'd just been caught doing something wrong. Norman walked over to Lilly and gave her a hug.

"Did you get out of school early?" Norman asked Lilly.

"Norman, I wasn't at school," she told him.

"What?" he asked her. "Where were you then?"

"Norman," Arthur said standing up and walking over to him. "You need to know that Lilly is not really your cousin."

"Huh, what are you saying?"

"She is actually Princess Lilliana, the heir to the throne of the four elements. She will be crowned queen soon enough."

Norman took a step back in total shock. He looked at his cousin, who was actually the princess. She suddenly didn't look the same to him anymore. Physically she looked the same but now she just looked different to Norman.

"How?" Norman asked.

"Nora is a guardian for the Golden Arrows. I was placed with her in secrecy for my protection until I turned five hundred and could be crowned," Lilliana told him.

"You're five hundred years old?" Norman gasped.

"Norman, we must get going," she said and turned to hug her guardian Nora goodbye. After which, Arthur and Norman gave a hug to Nora, then they grabbed their gear to get going. They all made their way over to the SUV parked in the driveway.

"Nice car, Uncle Arthur," Norman said.

"Thanks, buddy," Arthur said as they jumped into the SUV. Norman slid into the back and let the two of them sit up front. Suddenly the passenger door in the back opened up and a short, fat and hairy dwarf slid into the back seat.

"What are you?" Norman asked the dwarf.

"My name is Günter," the dwarf snorted at Norman."What are you?"

"Uhm…Norman."

"Are you sure?" Günter asked.

"Where did you come from?" Lilliana asked.

"I was living in the shed."

"You were living in our shed!" Norman almost shouted. "Wait a minute, I was just in the shed two days ago. I mowed the lawn and I definitely didn't see you in there when I was getting the lawnmower."

"Well to be exact I was living *under* the shed."

"Where do you think you are going?" Arthur asked.

"Well, with you, of course."

"We don't need you to come with us," Arthur told him.

"Of course you do, I'm the greatest guide the San Bernardino Mountains has ever seen," Günter insisted.

"That would be useful if we were heading in that direction, but we are going to Banff, not the San Bernardino Mountains," Arthur said.

"You see, that's why you need me."

"Okay, Günter, I'll bite," Lilliana said, "why do we need you?"

“Well because without the key to open the door in Banff you will never get in, and the key is in the San Gorgonio Mountain. Which is in the San Bernardino Mountains,” Günter said, crossing his arms and sitting back in the seat while he nodded in arrogance.

Arthur looked at him and then over to Princess Lilliana. She just looked out the window and shrugged. Norman was just sitting in the back smiling to himself. Arthur watched him through the rearview mirror.

“What is it, Norman?” Arthur asked.

“This is awesome,” Norman said. “I am actually sitting in the back of a SUV with a real live dwarf.”

“Big deal,” Günter said with a shrug, “you could be stuck next to a troll or worse yet, a human,” the dwarf said with a smile.

Arthur turned around to watch where he was going while he backed up out of the driveway. He pulled into the street and put the car into drive. As they pulled away he looked back at Norman.

“Nothing’s normal anymore, Norman,” his uncle said with a wink.

www.ingramcontent.com/pod-product-compliance
Lightning Source LLC
Chambersburg PA
CBHW020947310726
48980CB00001B/86

* 9 7 8 0 9 8 6 2 2 7 0 0 4 *